THE UNDERDOGS

Mariano Azuela

THE UNDERDOGS

A Novel of the Mexican Revolution

*A new rendition, with Notes, by Beth E. Jörgensen,
based on the E. Munguía, Jr., translation*

Introduction by Ilán Stavans

THE MODERN LIBRARY

NEW YORK

2002 Modern Library Paperback Edition

Introduction copyright © 2002 by Ilán Stavans
Revisions to the translation, and Notes, copyright © 2002 by Random House, Inc.

LIBRARY OF CONGRESS CATALOGING-IN-PUBLICATION DATA
Azuela, Mariano, 1873–1952.
[Los de abajo. English]
The underdogs: a novel of the Mexican Revolution /
Mariano Azuela; translated by E. Munguía, Jr.; revised, with notes,
by Beth E. Jörgensen;
with an introduction by Ilán Stavans.
p.   cm.
Includes bibliographical references.
ISBN 0-375-75942-5
1. Mexico—History—Revolution, 1910–1920—Fiction.   I. Munguía, E.
(Enrique), b. 1903.
II. Jörgensen, Beth E.   III. Title.
PQ7297.A9 L614   2002
863'.62—dc21   2002019640

Modern Library website address: www.modernlibrary.com

Printed in the United States of America

6   8   9   7

Contents

INTRODUCTION

Ilán Stavans

In a passage toward the end of Mariano Azuela's *The Underdogs* that is famous for its allegorical impregnation, Demetrio Macías, the protagonist, reappears in Limón, his small *rancho,* after an absence of two years. During this period, the revolution he was swept up in has been his sole raison d'être. He has fought in the ranks of Pancho Villa—"the Mexican Napoleon"—and has been persuaded that centuries of societal inequality in Mexico are likely to be abolished once and for all, if not for everyone, at least for *campesinos* who, like Demetrio, were destined to become generals in the insurgent army. Demetrio has learned to loot and slaughter, which is what war teaches men to do, but he has also inadvertently become a marionette of politicos who use the masses for their own advantage. "How beautiful the Revolution is," a soldier announces, "even in its very barbarity!"

It might indeed be beautiful, but Demetrio by then is tired of it, ready to move on. But when the time comes to surrender his weapons, he fails to do so, a decision that comes to the reader as a surprise of sorts; the domestic realm entices him, but apparently not enough. Instead, he decides to leave his family again and return to the battlefield. His wife, at his side near a canyon in that memorable scene, clearly baffled by this second departure, asks why. "Why do you keep on fighting, Demetrio?" He frowns deeply, then absentmindedly picks up a stone, which he throws to the bottom of the canyon, staring pensively into the abyss as he studies the arc of its flight.

La piedra . . . The stone is a symbol of Demetrio's incapacity to emerge clearheaded from the strife that violently catapulted Mexico into modernity. But it is also something else: an emblem of the nation's bottomward quest to institutionalize the turmoil that began in 1910 when the civilian Francisco I. Madero, under the banner *"Sufragio efectivo y no reelección,"* a statement that stood for a campaign that was in favor of accountable vote and against reelection, brought down the thirty-plus-year tyrannical regime of Porfirio Díaz. It was the beginning of a journey that, in less than two decades, included the assassinations of figures such as Emiliano Zapata, Venustiano Carranza, Alvaro Obregón, and Villa himself, who turned the revolution into a single-party autocracy. Mario Vargas Llosa, the Peruvian author of *The War of the End of the World,* once described it as "the perfect dictatorship," whose existence spanned the years from 1929 to 2000 and at the dawn of the new millennium, encompassed over a hundred million people. The party's name was Partido Revolucionario Institucional, a.k.a. PRI. In and of itself, the party's name is an oxymoron: might change be legislated, enforced? Just like the Bolsheviks in faraway Russia, the PRI members figured out a lucrative way to make the oxymoron a form of life.

Azuela's novel is a masterpiece of human compassion and narrative economy. Its overall value, I dare to suggest, rests on the effect of this pristine scene between Demetrio and his wife, which, in some metaphysical fashion, justifies the entire narrative endeavor. So much so that one might say *The Underdogs* was written so that this almost mythological exchange, this tête-à-tête between them—or better, between Demetrio's brighter and darker sides—could find its rightful loci. It might seem incongruous to some, and unfair, too, to ascribe to a single scene almost eighty years of ideological stagnation. Yet unquestionably the book is infused with a prophetic tone; therein, among other reasons, is why it has remained so popular over time. Encoded in the answer that Demetrio delivers to his wife is the fate of democracy and critical thought in Mexico. For he knows nothing about Adam Smith and Diderot, nor has he ever heard of Lenin. He is unacquainted with the larger intellectual debates of his age, is one of the countless anonymous individuals who make H-i-s-t-o-r-y without the faintest clue as to how to spell the word. Others more seasoned in arms and letters, personified in the book by Luis Cervantes (his patronymic, an oblique reference to the author of *Don Quixote,* cannot be sheer accident), will spell it out for Demetrio.

Mariano Azuela (1873–1952) knew everything about the spinning of stones. A liberal by faith and a doctor by profession, he was, like his protagonist, from a small village, Lagos de Moreno, in the state of Jalisco. He moved to Guadalajara, an urban center, to study medicine, and supported Madero in his quest to unseat Díaz. Azuela's Maderismo paid off when he was named director of education of his home state, but when the elected president was assassinated, thus igniting the chaos that came to be known as "la revolución mexicana," Azuela, too, joined the Villistas, as a doctor. The commitment allowed him to see the tragedy from the trenches in a way that, to me, at least, recalls the itinerary of Isaac Babel's in *Red Cavalry.* His first literary sketches, published in a newspaper of the country's capital, and influenced by his experience as an internist, date back to 1896. His influences were Edmond de Goncourt, Abbé Prevost, and, in particular, Alexandre Dumas's *La Dame aux camélias.* In the next ten years he drafted a series of flawed narratives, one of them prophetically titled *Los fracasados* (1908), roughly translatable as "the damned."

His staunch enemy was intolerance, religious and ideological. He witnessed the federal army fight the Villistas in Zacatecas. He served as a doctor in the battalion of Julián Medina, a significant model for Demetrio Macías. Eventually, Azuela rose to lieutenant colonel and medical staff director of the Estado Mayor. Nevertheless, it was intolerance that forced him into exile in El Paso, Texas, when the counterrevolutionary forces of Victoriano Huerta seized power. Exile might be a tuner for the soul. He, for one, used it as a springboard to reflect on the disaster of an uprising that had used human beings as peons. It was in El Paso that, around 1915, Azuela serialized his novel in a newspaper, *El Paso del Norte*. The circulation was approximately one thousand, and the author was paid three dollars a week during the period of serialization. In book form, the volume, 143 pages in length, was released a year later with the subtitle *Cuadernos y escenas de la revolución mexicana* (Notebooks and Scenes of the Mexican Revolution). Shortly after, Azuela moved to Mexico's capital, where he continued to write until the conclusion of his days, releasing on average a book every year, including novels, collections of stories, and volumes of essays. He practiced medicine among the poor in the northern neighborhoods of the expanding metropolis. He is buried in the most renowned of cemeteries, where dignitaries are honored in immortality: the Rotonda de los Hombres Ilustres.

That immortality Azuela owes solely to *The Underdogs*, though. Perhaps this is because no other work of his is so discerning, so perspicacious, yet so autobiographical. He seems to fully understand the inner and outer route of his characters; still, he allows them to engage in spontaneity, to seek their own path in the turmoil that surrounds them. Every syllable of their dialogue rings true. The battle sequences are startling, and so is the theater of sexes in which Macías's soldiers perform. What qualifies a work as a literary classic is its ability to survive rereadings, and *The Underdogs* does. Intriguingly, its publication went unnoticed for almost a decade. It wasn't reissued with significant emendations until 1925, and it wasn't until then that it became a critical and popular success. The delay is explainable: Mexico needed to process its internal turmoil, to seek a peaceful, stabilized form of government; also, artists and intellectuals required the type of wisdom that only time might offer. Not long after the novel was canonized, the PRI began its enduring rule. In any case, the volume is required reading in Mexican schools today and is celebrated as the apex of the tradition known as "novela de la revolución mexicana." Other quintessential authors in this tradition are Martín Luis Guzmán, responsible for *The Eagle* *and the Serpent,* as well as José Vasconcelos, Gregorio López y Fuentes, and Agustín Yáñez. Juan Rulfo and Carlos Fuentes also belong to it, for this tradition, over time, has replicated itself in myriad forms and inseminated almost every aspect of Mexican letters. Azuela is the undisputed leader of it: in commentaries of the twenties in *El Universal,* it was established that "what Diego Rivera is to painting, Azuela is to fiction." Intellectuals such as Rafael López Velarde and Julio Jiménez Rueda model him as a distilled, incisive author, *un futuro gran novelista* in whose pen lies our understanding of a rebellion that changes the country forever.*

The actual Spanish title is more poetic than the choice by E. Munguía, Jr., used in his English-language translation when it was published by Brentano's in 1929, just four years after the publication of Azuela's original "official" version. (The translation included engravings by José Clemente Orozco.) Its title, a reference to those who are victims of injustice, might lead some to believe the volume is about an American Dream of sorts. Nothing is further from the truth. There is no equivalent to the American Dream south of the border, where society is far more rigid, precluding, or at least obstructing, attempts at mobility across classes. *Los de abajo* means "the people beneath," "those from below"—or, in a politicized twist, the lumpen proletariat, and even perhaps, à la Victor Hugo, *les misérables.* In truth, proletariat is an erroneous reference, for Azuela's plot takes place in the countryside, among destitute *campesinos,* which was the constituency, as it were, at the forefront of the revolution. And it is also significant, in my eyes, that *The Underdogs* was first published in the United States. It isn't possible to describe Azuela as part of the Chicano tradition, for he never became

* *The Underdogs* is the subject of an unfortunate 117-minute-long film adaptation, financed by the Instituto Mexicano de Cinematografía in 1977, directed by Servando González, photographed by Angel Bilbatúa, with Eric del Castillo, Enrique Lucero, and Gloria Mestre. It belongs to the so-called "infamous period" in Mexico's movie industry. Even the production summary is nefarious: "A violent, passionate, and brutal chronicle of the Mexican Revolution and of Mexican history. In the midst of misery and injustice appeared the face of *Los de abajo,* and the feast of those in power became a bloody and destructive orgy."

an émigré. Instead, he is an *exile*, defined by the *Oxford English Dictionary* as "a banished person," e.g., "one compelled to reside away from his native land." Azuela profited from a renewed perspective on his experiences in the battlefield: his was a fatalistic viewpoint with an aesthetic force that allows the reader to see destruction from within, not only from without. In fact, his is a style that recalls the Cossack stories of Isaac Babel in *Red Cavalry*, authentic gems where the parsimony of language and the restraint of emotions give place to a sense of desolation. (Babel's "Story of My Dovecote," by the way, includes a scene where a stone on the ground becomes equally emblematic.) The empathy I find between them is not accidental. One might argue that Mexico and Russia shared much in the early days of the twentieth century, which could explain why these were the first two countries submerged in social upheavals. These upheavals left an imprint on their respective literatures. For instance, the fatalism of Azuela and the bleak state in which the lower class finds itself trapped recall similar patterns in Maxim Gorky, and the attention paid by the Mexican to "the small details of life" and even his misleading tenderness bring to mind Anton Chekhov.

Azuela's rendezvous in English are of interest to me. *The Underdogs* has been rendered into more than a dozen languages, including Serbian, Japanese, and Yiddish. But he has done superbly in English. Four other novels by him have been translated into Shakespeare's tongue: *Marcela* (1932), *The Flies* and *The Bosses* (both 1956), and *The Trials of a Respectable Family* (1963). As for his masterpiece, there are, to my knowledge, a total of four English translations: the other three are by Frances Kellam Hendricks and Beatrice Berler (1963); Stanley Linn Robe (1979); and Frederick H. Fornoff (1992). But Munguía's is unquestionably the most agile, although it takes unnecessary liberties. For instance, the translator attempts to re-create the jargon of the lower class by equating it to the language of an American black. This is clear midway in the plot line, at the moment when the character of Meco finds out that in his absence his wife has delivered another baby. In Spanish, Azuela writes: *"Oye, Pancracio . . . En carta que me pone mi mujer me notifica que izque ya ten-*

emos otro hijo. ¿Cómo es eso? ¡Yo no la veo dende tiempos del siñor Madero!"
Of course, Mexicanisms such as *"izque"* and *"dende tiempos del siñor"*
are nightmarish to render with a degree of accuracy. Munguía re-
duces the resonance thus: "Hey, Pancracio . . . my wife writes me
I've got another kid. How in hell is that? I ain't seen her since
Madero was President." A few lines later, Meco sings what Azuela
describes as *"horrible falsete,"* which in English becomes a song "in a
voice horribly shrill":

> Yo le daba un centavo
> Y ella me dijo que no . . .
> Yo le daba medio
> Y no lo quiso agarrar.
> Tanto me estuvo rogando
> Hasta que me sacó un rial.
> ¡Ay, qué mujeres ingratas,
> no saben considerar!

Munguía takes the lyric out of context, yet registers the pathos of
the original:

> I gave her a penny
> That wasn't enough
> I gave her a nickel
> The wench wanted more
> We bargained. I asked
> If a dime was enough
> But she wanted a quarter
> By God! That was tough!
> All wenches are fickle

This tergiversation and others similar in tone might have
eclipsed, partially, Azuela's talents. Every translation places a veil
on the original, but have the author's colors in this case become too
mitigated, too contorted? In her revision of Munguía's translation,
Beth E. Jörgensen of the University of Rochester has gone back to
Azuela's original (specifically, to the edition of 1927, published in

Jalapa, Veracruz), in order to replace Munguía's stylistic liberties with her own (see page 52).

A painstaking comparison of Azuela's *Los de abajo* and Munguía's *The Underdogs* evidences the obvious: the latter is as wordy as it is weighty. Jörgensen has caught small typical mistakes, such as the misidentification of the subject of verbs, the misattribution of dialogue, and some lexical inaccuracies. The majority of her changes have to do with style, though. She has reinstated the original division of paragraphs, returned to Azuela's interjection of episodes narrated in the present tense, reduced rhetorical flourishes, and fought against Munguía's dated English ("on the morrow," instead of "the next morning"). She is consistent with names, too. Munguía, for instance, corrected *Carranzo* to *Carranza* at a point in which Azuela wanted to highlight the ignorance of one of his characters; Jörgensen has granted us that ignorance again. And why did Munguía change *Codorniz* for *Quail* but left *Manteca* alone? Jörgensen reverts this trend, then inserts endnotes to explain what the names evoke. Her use of endnotes might be deemed too academic by some; it indicates a difference in readership: Munguía targeted his work to a general audience, Jörgensen to the curious student.

In the end, the three versions at hand are dramatically different. Consider the following comparison of Part 1, Chapter 2:

Azuela: *"Cerca de ellos estaba, en montón, la piel dorada de una res, sobre la tierra húmeda de sangre."*

Munguía: "The rays of the sun, falling about them, cast a golden radiance over the bloody hide of a calf, lying on the ground nearby."

Jörgensen: "Close by, the golden hide of a calf lay in a heap on the blood-soaked earth."

Translations go in and out of fashion, whereas the author's source remains, magically, fossilized in a state of grace. The attempt to "reclaim" an established translation, to appropriate it, to bring it back to life, isn't scandalous. It is a trend in the history of literature.

(In English alone, the hunger to reprint *Don Quixote de la Mancha* has resulted in the careless manipulation of translations by Shelton [1612], Motteux [1700], Jarvis [1742], and Smollett [1755].) Perhaps the future will condemn Jörgensen's excess of simplicity, but to us today it is an honorable approach: it allows for a revaluation of Azuela's talents. Those talents are best perceived in the symmetry he builds between freedom and determinism, a feature I find admirable every time I reopen *The Underdogs.* Harriet de Onís once questioned if, at heart, its author was a reactionary. After all, he rushed to join the revolution but withdrew from it just as fast. Reactionaries produce nihilistic literature; Azuela, on the other hand, was a moralist: his novel is about ethical choices. The clash between the individual and the community, between one's private aspirations and those of the entire nation, is brilliantly explored. Demetrio devotes his energy to a righteous cause, and for it he is promised a better future. But he is a man left to fend for himself. And it is that test that he fails. The novel is about the benevolence of Mexicans, but also about their docility. Hence, Azuela allows us an invaluable glimpse into his nation's psyche. At one point the urbane Cervantes tells Demetrio straightforwardly: "You rose up to protest against the evils of all the *caciques* who are ruining the whole nation. . . . We are the tools Destiny makes use of to reclaim the sacred rights of the people."

Las herramientas del destino—the tools of destiny? Again, it is in that fateful scene, as the stone spins down into the abyss, that everything comes into focus. "Look at that stone," Demetrio asserts, "how it keeps on going. . . ."

ILÁN STAVANS is the Lewis-Sebring Professor in Latin American and Latino Culture at Amherst College. His books include *The Hispanic Condition, Art and Anger, The Riddle of Cantinflas,* and *On Borrowed Words: A Memoir of Language.* He is the editor of *The Oxford Book of Jewish Stories.* His work has been translated into half a dozen languages.

PART ONE

"How beautiful the Revolution is, even in its very barbarity!"
Solís said with deep feeling.

I

"That's no animal, I tell you!... Listen to Palomo barking! It *must* be a human being."

The woman stared into the darkness of the sierra.

"What if they're Federals?"[1] said a man who sat squatting and eating, a coarse earthenware plate in his right hand, three folded tortillas in the other.

The woman made no answer; all her senses were directed outside the hut.

The beat of horses' hoofs rang in the quarry nearby. Palomo barked again, louder and more angrily.

"Well, Demetrio, I think you had better hide, all the same."

Stolidly, the man finished eating; he reached for a water jug and gulped down the water in it. Then he stood up.

"Your rifle is under the mat," she whispered.

A tallow candle illumined the small room. In one corner stood a plow, a yoke, a goad, and other agricultural implements. An old adobe mold hung by ropes from the roof and served as a bed; on it a child slept, covered with rags.

Demetrio buckled his cartridge belt about his waist and picked up his rifle. Tall and well built, with a sanguine, beardless face, he wore shirt and trousers of white cloth, a broad-brimmed straw hat, and leather sandals.

With slow, measured step, he left the room, vanishing into the impenetrable darkness of the night.

Palomo, excited to the point of fury, had jumped over the corral fence. Suddenly a shot rang out. The dog moaned, then barked no more.

Men on horseback rode up, shouting and swearing. Two of them dismounted, while the other hung back to watch the horses.

"Hey, there, woman, we want food! Eggs, milk, beans, anything you've got! We're starving!"

"Damned sierra! It would take the Devil himself not to lose his way!"

"Sergeant, even the Devil would go astray if he were as drunk as you are."

One of them wore chevrons on his shoulders, the other red stripes on his sleeves.

"Whose place is this, old woman? . . . What the . . . Isn't anybody home?"

"What about that light and that child there? Look here, woman, we want to eat, and damn quick, too! Are you coming out, or are we going to make you?"

"You swine! You've gone and killed my dog! What harm did he ever do you? What did you have against *him*, poor little Palomo!"

The woman reentered the house, dragging the dog behind her, very white and fat, with lifeless eyes and limp body.

"Look at those cheeks, Sergeant! Don't get riled, light of my life: I swear I'll turn your home into a dovecote, see? But by God!

> "Don't look so haughty, dear,
> Banish all fear
> Look at me lovingly
> Light of my eyes."

The officer finished singing in his tipsy voice.

"Tell me what they call this ranch, woman?" the sergeant asked.

"Limón," the woman replied curtly, carrying wood to the fire and fanning the coals.

"So we're in Limón, eh, the famous Demetrio Macías's country, eh? ... Do you hear that, Lieutenant? We're in Limón."

"Limón? What the hell do I care? If I'm bound for hell, Sergeant, I might as well go there now ... now that I have such a good mount. Look at the cheeks on that darling, look at them! There's a pair of ripe red apples for a fellow to bite into!"

"I'll wager you know that bandit, lady. . . . I was in the pen with him at Escobedo."

"Bring me a bottle of tequila, Sergeant; I've decided to spend the night with this little brunette. . . . What's that? The colonel? ... Why talk about the colonel now? He can go straight to hell. And if he doesn't like it, it's all right with me. Come on, Sergeant, tell the corporal outside to unsaddle the horses and feed them. I'll stay here. Listen, my girl, you let the sergeant fry the eggs and warm up the tortillas; you come here to me. See this wallet full of nice new bills? They're all for you, darling. Sure, I want you to have them. Imagine! I'm drunk, see, a little, and that's why I'm kind of hoarse. . . . I left half my gullet down Guadalajara way, and I've been spitting the other half out all the way up here. Oh, well, who cares? But I want you to have that money. Hey, Sergeant, where's my bottle? Darling, you're awfully far away. Come closer and pour yourself a drink. You won't, eh? Afraid of your ... er ... husband ... or whatever he is? Well, if he's skulking in some hole, you tell him to come out. What the hell do I care? I'm not scared of rats, see!"

Suddenly a white shadow loomed on the dark threshold.

"Demetrio Macías!" the sergeant cried as he stepped back in terror.

The lieutenant stood up, silent, cold, and motionless as a statue.

"Shoot them!" the woman cried, her throat dry.

"Oh, excuse us, friend ... I didn't know. . . . But I respect a truly brave man."

Demetrio stood his ground, looking them up and down, an insolent and disdainful smile wrinkling his face.

"Yes, I not only respect them, but I like them. Here's my hand on it, friend to friend . . . That's all right, Demetrio Macías, you don't want to shake hands. . . . It's because you don't know me, it's because you see me doing this dog's job. . . . But what do you want, friend? I'm poor, I have a big family to support! . . . Sergeant, let's go; I always respect the home of a brave man, a real man!"

When they had gone, the woman drew close to Demetrio.

"Holy Virgin of Jalpa,[2] what a scare! I thought it was you they'd shot."

"You go to my father's house, quick!" Demetrio ordered.

She wanted to hold him in her arms; she entreated, she wept. But he pushed away from her gently and replied in a somber voice.

"I've an idea the whole lot of them are coming."

"Why didn't you kill them?"

"Their hour hasn't struck yet."

They went out together; she bore the child in her arms. At the door they separated, moving off in opposite directions.

The moon peopled the mountain with vague shadows. In every crag and in every scrub oak tree, Demetrio could see the poignant silhouette of a woman with a child in her arms.

When, after many hours of climbing, he gazed back, huge flames shot up from the depths of the canyon by the river. His house was on fire. . . .

II

Everything was still swathed in shadows as Demetrio Macías began his descent to the bottom of the ravine. His path was a narrow ledge, along a cliff, between giant rocks striped with huge, eroded cracks, and a drop-off hundreds of meters deep that looked as if it had been cut with a single stroke.

During his rapid, agile descent, he mused:

"The Federals will surely find our track now and chase us down like dogs. It's a good thing they don't know the trails and paths up here.... But if they got someone from Moyahua to guide them ... because all the men from Limón or Santa Rosa or the other nearby ranches are on our side, and they wouldn't hand us over. That *cacique*[1] who's chased me and run me ragged over these hills is at Moyahua now; he'd give his eyeteeth to see me dangling from a telegraph pole with my tongue sticking out of my mouth...."

And he reached the bottom of the ravine just as dawn was breaking. He lay on the rocks and fell asleep.

The river crept along, murmuring as the waters rose and fell in small cascades. Birds chirped from their hiding places among the pitahayas,[2] and the monotonous, eternal drone of the cicadas filled the rocky solitude with mystery.

Demetrio woke with a start, waded across the river, and headed up the opposite side of the gorge. He climbed the crags laboriously as an ant, gripping rocks and branches with his hands, clutching every stone in the trail with his bare feet.

When he reached the summit, the sun was bathing the high plateau in a lake of gold. Near the canyon, enormous rocks loomed like fantastic African skulls; the pitahaya trees rose like the gnarled fingers of a giant; trees stretched toward the pit of the abyss. Amid the stark rocks and dry branches, St. John's roses bloomed like a white offering to the sun, as it unraveled its golden threads, one by one, from rock to rock.

Demetrio stopped at the summit, reached with his right arm, drew the horn that hung on his back, held it up to his thick lips, and, swelling his cheeks, blew three loud blasts. From beyond the next summit, three whistles answered his signal.

In the distance, from a conical heap of reeds and dry straw, man after man emerged, one after the other, their naked legs and chests polished as dark as old bronze.

They rushed up to greet Demetrio.

"They've burned my house down," he replied to their inquisitive looks.

There were curses, threats, and insults.

Demetrio let their anger run its course; then he drew a bottle from under his shirt, took a long swig, wiped it with the back of his hand, and passed it around. The bottle went from mouth to mouth until not a drop was left. The men licked their lips greedily.

"God willing," said Demetrio, "tomorrow or this very night we'll meet the Federals face to face. What do you say, boys, shall we let them find their way around these trails?"

The half-naked crew jumped to their feet, uttering shrill cries of joy. Then they gave vent to more insults, oaths, and threats.

"Of course, we can't tell how strong they are," Demetrio remarked, as his glance traveled over their faces. "Julián Medina[3] at Hostotipaquillo, with a half dozen men and knives that they sharpened on a grindstone, faced up to the police and the Federals in the town, and threw them out. . . ."

"We're every bit as good as Medina's crowd!" said a broad-shouldered man with a black beard, bushy eyebrows, and a sweet look in his eyes.

"All I can say," he added, "is that if I'm not the owner of a Mauser, cartridge belt, trousers, and shoes by tomorrow evening, my name's not Anastasio Montañez. . . . Look here, Codorniz,[4] you don't believe me, do you? I have a dozen bullets in me. . . . Demetrio will vouch for that. . . . I'm about as afraid of bullets as I am of caramel candy. What do you mean you don't believe me?"

"Viva Anastasio Montañez!" shouted Manteca.

"No," answered Montañez. "Viva Demetrio Macías, our chief, and long live God in His heaven and the Virgin Mary."

"Viva Demetrio Macías!" they all shouted.

They built a fire with dry brush and wood and placed chunks of fresh meat upon the burning coals. As the blaze rose, they encircled the fire, sat on their heels, and inhaled the odor of the meat as it twisted and crackled on the embers.

Close by, the golden hide of a calf lay in a heap on the blood-soaked earth. Meat dangled from a rope fastened between two huisache trees, to dry in the sun and wind.

"Well," Demetrio said, "you know we've only twenty rifles, besides my thirty-thirty. If there are just a few of them, we'll shoot until there's not a man left alive. If there are a lot of 'em, we can give 'em a good scare, anyhow."

He undid a belt about his waist, loosened a knot in it, and offered the contents to his companions.

"Salt!" A murmur of approbation rose among them as each took a few grains between the tips of his fingers.

They ate voraciously; then, glutted, lay down on the ground, facing the sky, and sang monotonous, sad songs, uttering a strident shout after each stanza.

III

In the brush and foliage of the sierra, Demetrio Macías and his twenty-five men slept until the sound of the horn, blown by Pancracio from the crest of a peak, awakened them.

"It's time, boys! Get ready!" said Anastasio Montañez, examining his rifle springs.

But another hour elapsed with no sound save the song of the locust in the brush and the croaking of the frog in his mud hole.

At last, when the faint rays of the moon faded in the rosy dimness of the dawn, the first silhouette of a soldier loomed at the highest point of the trail. Behind him, others appeared, ten more, one hundred more; but suddenly, darkness swallowed them up. Only when the sun rose could they see that the canyon was alive with men: midgets seated on miniature horses.

"Look how pretty!" cried Pancracio. "Come on, boys, let's go and have fun with them!"

Now the moving dwarf figures were lost in the dense chaparral; now they reappeared, stark and black against the ocher rocks.

The voices of officers and soldiers were clearly audible.

Demetrio raised his hand: their rifle locks clicked.

"Fire!" he ordered in a low voice.

Twenty-one men shot as one; twenty-one Federals fell off their horses. Caught by surprise, the rest of the column halted, etched like bas-reliefs in the stone.

Another volley, and a score of soldiers tumbled down from rock to rock, heads split open.

"Come out, bandits. Come out, you starved dogs!"

"Kill the corn thieves!"

"Kill the cattle rustlers! . . ."

The soldiers shouted defiance at their enemies, who, motionless and silent in their hiding places, were content to show off the marksmanship that had already made them famous.

"Look, Pancracio," said Meco, his face completely black except for his eyes and teeth. "This is for the man who's going to pass that tree. Son of a . . . Take that! Right in the head! Did you see that? . . . Now one for the fellow on the dappled horse. Down you go, you bald bastard!"

"I'll give that lad on the trail's edge a shower of lead. If you don't hit the river, I'm a liar! How's that! . . . Did you see?"

"Oh, come on, Anastasio, don't be cruel; lend me your rifle! Come on, one shot, just one!"

Manteca, Codorniz, and the other unarmed men begged for a gun, imploring permission to fire at least a shot apiece.

"Come out of your holes if you've got any guts!"

"Show your faces, you lousy cowards!"

From peak to peak, the shouts were heard distinctly as though uttered across a street.

Suddenly, Codorniz stood up, naked, holding his trousers as though he were a bullfighter flaunting a red cape at the Federals. A shower of shots sprayed Demetrio's men.

"God! That was like a hornet's nest buzzing overhead," said Anastasio Montañez, lying flat on the ground without daring to look up.

"Codorniz, you son of a bitch, you stay where I told you," growled Demetrio.

They crawled to take new positions.

The Federals, congratulating themselves on their successes, had ceased firing when another volley roused them.

"More coming!" shouted the soldiers.

Some, panic-stricken, turned their horses back; others, abandoning their mounts, began to climb up the mountain and seek shelter behind the rocks. The officers had to shoot at the fleeing soldiers to restore order.

"Down there, down there!" yelled Demetrio as he pointed his thirty-thirty at the translucent thread of the river.

A soldier fell into the water; at each shot, invariably, another one bit the dust. But only Demetrio was shooting toward the river, and for every soldier he killed, ten or twenty of them climbed unharmed up the other side.

"Fire on the ones down there . . . *los de abajo,*" he screamed with fury.

Now his fellows were exchanging rifles, and making wagers on their marksmanship.

"My leather belt if I don't hit that one on the black horse in the head. Lend me your rifle, Meco. . . ."

"Twenty Mauser cartridges and a half yard of sausage if you let me spill that lad riding the bay mare. All right! . . . Now! See him jump! Like a bloody deer."

"Don't run, you half-breeds. Come along with you! Come and meet Father Demetrio!"

Now it was Demetrio's men who screamed insults. Pancracio, his smooth face swollen in exertion, yelled his lungs out. Manteca roared, the veins and muscles in his neck dilated, his murderous eyes narrowed to two slits.

Demetrio fired shot after shot, constantly warning his men of impending danger, but they took no heed until they felt the bullets spattering them from one side.

"They've branded me!" Demetrio cried, his teeth clenched. "Sons of a . . . !"

Then, very swiftly, he slid down a gully and was lost. . . .

IV

Two were missing, Serapio the candymaker, and Antonio, who played the cymbals in the Juchipila band.

"Maybe they'll join us farther on," said Demetrio.

The return journey proved moody. Anastasio Montañez alone preserved the sweet expression in his sleepy eyes and on his bearded face. And Pancracio retained the enduring repulsiveness of his jutting profile.

The soldiers had retreated; Demetrio was rounding up the horses that they had hidden in the sierra.

Suddenly Codorniz, who had been walking ahead, called out. He had caught sight of his missing companions swinging from the branches of a mesquite. They were Serapio and Antonio. Everyone recognized them, and Anastasio Montañez muttered a prayer:

"Our Father Who art in heaven, hallowed be Thy name."

"Amen," the others answered in low tones, their heads bowed, their hats upon their breasts. . . .

Then, hurriedly, they took the Juchipila canyon northward, without halting to rest until late into the evening.

Codorniz kept walking close to Anastasio, unable to banish from his mind the two who were hanged, their limp necks, the dangling arms, their stiff legs softly rocked by the wind.

The next day, Demetrio complained bitterly of his w could no longer ride on horseback. They were forced to c *l. He* the rest of the way on a makeshift stretcher of leaves and b *him*

"You're bleeding badly, compadre," said Anastasio Mont. tearing off one of his shirtsleeves and tying it tightly ab Demetrio's thigh, a little above the wound.

"That's good," said Venancio. "That will stop the bleeding and relieve the pain."

Venancio was a barber. In his hometown, he pulled teeth and applied plasters and leeches. He enjoyed a certain prestige because he had read *The Wandering Jew* and *The May Sun*.[1] They called him "Doctor"; and since he was conceited about his knowledge, he was a man of very few words.

They took turns carrying the stretcher, in relays of four, over the bare, stony mesa and up the steep passes.

At high noon, when the hazy, acrid heat was suffocating and their eyesight was blurred, they heard the rhythmic, monotonous moan of the wounded man together with the unceasing song of the locusts.

They stopped to rest at every small hut they found hidden among the steep, jagged rocks.

"Thank God, a kind soul and a tortilla full of beans and chili are never lacking," Anastasio Montañez said with a belch.

The mountainfolk would shake callused hands with the travelers and exclaim:

"May God bless you! May God help you and lead you to safety! . . . Today it's you, but tomorrow we're also leaving here, fleeing the draft, chased down by those damned government people who've declared a fight to the death against all us poor folks. They steal our pigs, our chickens, and even our corn. They burn our houses and carry off our women, and if they ever get hold of us, they kill us on the spot like rabid dogs."

At sunset, amid the flames dyeing the sky with vivid colors, a group of houses appeared in a clearing in the heart of the blue mountains. Demetrio ordered them to carry him there.

These proved to be a few wretched straw huts, scattered along the riverbank, between rows of young corn and beans. They lowered the stretcher, and Demetrio, in a weak voice, asked for a drink of water.

In the dark openings of the huts, faded homespun dresses, bony chests, disheveled heads, and, behind them, shining eyes and ruddy cheeks were crowded together.

A child with a large belly and glossy dark skin came close to the stretcher to inspect the wounded man; then an old woman, and soon all of them drew about in a circle.

A kind young girl brought a gourd of water. Demetrio took the vessel in his trembling hands and drank greedily.

"Don't you want some more?"

He raised his eyes; the girl had ordinary features but her voice was very sweet.

Wiping his sweating brow with the back of his hand and turning on one side, he gasped:

"May God reward you."

Then his whole body shook, making the leaves and the legs of the stretcher rustle. The fever made him faint.

"It's a damp night and that's terrible for the fever," said Remigia, an old, wrinkled, barefooted woman, wearing a cloth rag for a blouse.

She invited them to move Demetrio into her hut.

Pancracio, Anastasio Montañez, and Codorniz lay down beside the stretcher like faithful dogs, watchful of their master's wishes.

The rest scattered about in search of food.

Remigia offered them all she had: chili and tortillas.

"Imagine! I had eggs, chickens, even a goat and her kid, but those damn Federals cleaned me out."

Then, cupping her hands around her mouth, she drew near Anastasio and murmured in his ear:

"Imagine, they even carried away Señora Nieves's little girl! . . ."

V

Waking up with a start, Codorniz opened his eyes and stood up.

"Montañez, did you hear? . . . A shot! . . . Montañez! Hey, wake up!"

He shook him vigorously until Montañez moved and stopped snoring.

"What in the name of . . . Now you're at it again. . . . I tell you there's no such thing as ghosts," Anastasio muttered out of a half-sleep.

"I heard a shot, Montañez."

"Go back to sleep, Codorniz, or I'll bust your nose."

"No, Anastasio, I tell you it's no nightmare. I've forgotten those fellows they hung, honest. It's a shot, all right; I heard it loud and clear."

"A shot, you say? Let's see, hand me my gun."

Anastasio Montañez rubbed his eyes, stretched out his arms and legs, and stood up lazily.

They left the hut. The sky was solid with stars; and the moon was rising like a sharp scythe. The confused sound of women crying in fright came from the huts; and they heard the rattle of the

guns of the men who had been sleeping in the open, and now woke
up, too.

"You fool! . . . You've smashed my foot!"

A voice rang clearly through the darkness.

"Who goes there?"

The shout echoed from rock to rock, through crests and hollows,
until it spent itself in the far, silent reaches of the night.

"Who goes there?" Anastasio repeated his challenge louder,
pulling back the lock of his Mauser.

"One of Demetrio's men," a voice answered from close by.

"It's Pancracio!" Codorniz cried joyfully. Relieved, he rested the
butt of his rifle on the ground.

Pancracio appeared, leading a young man covered with dust
from his felt hat to his coarse shoes. A fresh bloodstain lay on his
trousers close to his foot.

"Who's this *curro*?"[1] Anastasio asked.

"I'm on guard duty, and I heard a noise in the brush, and I
shouted, 'Who goes there?' and then this lad answered, 'Carranzo!
Carranzo!' I don't know anyone by that name, and so I says, 'Carranzo, hell!' and I just pumped a bit of lead into his hoof."

Smiling, Pancracio turned his beardless face around as if solicit-
ing applause.

Then the stranger spoke:

"Who's your commander?"

Proudly, Anastasio raised his head, went up to him, and looked
him in the face.

The stranger lowered his tone considerably.

"Well, I'm a revolutionary, too; the Federals drafted me and I
served as a private; but I managed to desert during the battle the
day before yesterday, and I've been walking about in search of you
all."

"So he's a Federal soldier, eh?" interrupted many of the men,
looking at him in astonishment.

"One of those damn *mochos*,"[2] said Anastasio Montañez. "Why
the hell didn't you pump your lead into his brain?"

"What's he talking about, anyhow? I can't make head or tail of it. He says he wants to see Demetrio and that he's got plenty to say to him. But don't worry, we've got plenty of time, so long as you're in no hurry," said Pancracio, loading his gun.

"What kind of brutes are you?" the stranger cried.

He could say no more because Anastasio's fist knocked him down, with his face covered in blood.

"Shoot the *mocho*!"

"Hang him!"

"Burn him alive; he's a Federal."

In great excitement, they yelled and shrieked and were about to fire at the prisoner.

"Sssh! Shut up! I think Demetrio's saying something," Anastasio said, striving to quiet them down. Indeed, Demetrio was trying to find out what was going on, and he ordered them to bring the prisoner before him.

"It's positively infamous, chief. Look at this!" Luis Cervantes said, pointing to the bloodstains on his trousers and to his bleeding face.

"Well, now, who in hell are you?" Demetrio asked.

"My name is Luis Cervantes. I'm a medical student and a journalist. I wrote a piece in favor of the revolution, and so they persecuted me, caught me, and finally landed me in the barracks." The tale of his adventure that he continued to spin in a melodramatic tone drew guffaws of mirth from Pancracio and Manteca.

"All I've tried to do is to make myself clear on this point. I want you to be convinced that I am truly one of your coreligionists. . . ."

"Co . . . what?" Demetrio asked, bringing his ear close to Cervantes.

"Coreligionists, chief, that is to say, I pursue the same ideals, and I defend the cause that you defend."

Demetrio smiled:

"What cause *are* we defending?"

Luis Cervantes, disconcerted, could find no reply.

"Look at that mug! . . . Why waste any time, Demetrio? Let's shoot him," Pancracio urged impatiently.

Demetrio touched a lock of hair that covered his ear, and scratched himself for a long time, lost in thought. Having found no solution, he said:

"Get out, all of you . . . it's aching again. . . . Anastasio, put out the candle. Lock him up in the corral and let Pancracio and Manteca watch him. Tomorrow, we'll see. . . ."

VI

Through the shadows of the starry night, Luis Cervantes had not yet managed to detect the exact shape of the objects about him, and seeking the most suitable resting place, he laid his weary bones down on a fresh pile of manure under the blurred mass of a huisache tree. He stretched out, more exhausted than resigned, and closed his eyes resolutely, determined to sleep until his fierce keepers awakened him, or the morning sun burned his ears. Something vaguely warm at his side, then a tired, hoarse breath, made him shudder; he unfolded his arms, and feeling about him with his hands, he touched the coarse hairs of a large pig, which, resenting the presence of a neighbor, began to grunt.

Now all of Luis's efforts to sleep proved quite useless, not only because of the pain of his wound or the bruises on his flesh but because of the immediate and exact recognition of his failure.

Yes: he hadn't learned in time to tell the difference between handling a scalpel, or fulminating against the thieving rebels in a small town newspaper, and setting out to hunt the rebels down, rifle in hand, in their own territory. During his first day's march as volunteer lieutenant—a brutal sixty miles' journey that left his hips and legs fused as if his bones had been soldered together—he had begun to suspect the error of his ways. A week later, after his first skirmish against the rebels, he understood every rule of the game. He would swear, with his hand placed on a crucifix, that when the soldiers raised their guns to their faces, some profoundly eloquent voice had spoken behind them, saying, "Run for your lives." It was all crystal clear. Even his noble-spirited horse, accustomed to battle, had turned tail and galloped furiously away, to stop only at a safe distance from the sound of gunfire. It was just at sunset, when the mountain began to fill with vague and restless shadows, when darkness quickly scaled the ramparts of the mountain. What could be more logical, then, than to seek refuge behind the rocks and attempt to sleep, granting mind and body a sorely needed rest? But the soldier's logic is the logic of absurdity. The next morning, for example, his colonel awakens him rudely out of his sleep, kicking him unmercifully, and drags him from his hiding place, with his face swollen from blows. The rest of the officers, moreover, burst into hilarious mirth and, laughing to the point of tears, beg the colonel to pardon the deserter. The colonel, therefore, instead of sentencing him to be shot, kicks him in the butt and assigns him to kitchen duty.

This signal insult was destined to bear poisonous fruit. Luis Cervantes decides to play turncoat, although just in his own mind for the time being. The sufferings of the underdogs, of the disinherited masses, touch him to the core; his cause is the sublime cause of the downtrodden who clamor for justice, only justice. He becomes the confidant of the humble footsoldier, and, why not!, he sheds tears of pity for a poor mule, dead from exhaustion after the torturous journey.

From then on, Luis Cervantes's prestige with the soldiers increased. Some actually dared to make rash confessions. One among them, conspicuous for his sobriety and silence, told him: "I'm a carpenter by trade; I had a mother, an old woman nailed to her chair for ten years by rheumatism. In the middle of the night, three policemen dragged me out of my house. I woke up a soldier, twenty-five miles away from my hometown. A month ago, our company passed by there again. My mother was already under the sod! . . . I was all she had in life. Now no one needs me. But, by God, I'm damned if I'll use these cartridges they make us carry, against the enemy. If a miracle happens (my Blessed Mother, the Virgin of Guadalupe,[1] grant me this favor), then I'll join Villa's men; and I swear by the holy soul of my old mother, that I'll make every one of these Federals pay."

Another soldier, a bright young fellow, but a charlatan at heart, a drunk and a pothead, called him aside, and eyeing him with a vague, glassy stare, whispered in his ear. "You know, partner . . . those men over there, you know who I mean . . . on the other side . . . they ride the best horses from up north and all over, and they harness their mounts with pure hammered silver. But us? Oh hell, we've got to ride plugs, that's all, and not one of them good enough to stagger round a water well. You see, don't you, partner? The men on the other side—they get shiny new silver coins; we get only lousy paper money printed in that murderer's factory. I tell you!"

The majority of the soldiers spoke in much the same tenor. Even a top sergeant candidly confessed, "Yes, I enlisted all right. But, by God, I missed the mark by a long shot. What you can't make in a lifetime, sweating like a mule and breaking your back, you can make in a few months just running around the sierra with a gun on your back. But not with this crowd, pal, not with this lousy outfit. . . ."

Luis Cervantes, who already shared this hidden, implacable, and mortal hatred of the noncommissioned and the commissioned officers, and of all his superiors, felt that a veil had been removed from his eyes; clearly, now, he saw the final outcome of the struggle.

And, yet, what had happened? The first moment he was able to join his coreligionists, instead of welcoming him with open arms, they threw him into a pigsty!

—

Day broke: the roosters crowed in the huts; the chickens, perched in the huisache tree, began to stretch their wings, shake their feathers, and fly down to the ground.

Cervantes saw his guards lying on top of a dung heap, snoring. In his imagination, he reviewed the features of the two men from last night. One, Pancracio, was pockmarked, freckled, beardless; a jutting chin, a receding forehead, ears close to his skull; a beastly-looking man. The other, Manteca, was so much human refuse; his eyes were almost hidden, his look sullen; his straight hair fell over his ears and forehead to his neck; his scrofulous lips hung eternally agape.

Once more, he felt his skin crawl.

VII

Still drowsy, Demetrio ran his hand through his curly, side-parted hair, which hung over his moist forehead, and opened his eyes.

Distinctly he heard the woman's melodious voice that he had already sensed in his dream, and he turned toward the door.

It was broad daylight; the rays of sunlight filtered through the thatch of the hut. The girl who had offered him that cold, delicious water the day before, the girl of whom he had dreamed all night long, entered the hut now, kindly and sweet as ever, carrying a pitcher of milk brimming over with foam.

"It's goat's milk, but it's very good. . . . Come on now, taste it."

Demetrio smiled gratefully, straightened up, grasped the clay pitcher, and began to drink the milk in little gulps, without taking his eyes off the girl.

She grew self-conscious, lowered her eyes.

"What's your name?"

"Camilla."

"I like that name, but I like your voice better."

Camilla blushed, and as he tried to seize her wrist, she grew frightened, picked up the empty pitcher, and flew out the door.

"No, compadre Demetrio," Anastasio Montañez commented gravely, "you've got to break them in first. Hmm! It's a hell of a lot of scars women have left on my body. I have a lot of experience in that...."

"I feel all right now, compadre." Demetrio pretended he had not heard him. "I was feverish and I sweated like a pig all night, but I feel refreshed today. The thing that's still killing me is that goddamn wound. Call Venancio to look after me."

"What are we going to do with the *curro* we caught last night?" Pancracio asked.

"That's right! I was forgetting all about him."

As usual, Demetrio hesitated a while before he reached a decision.

"Here, Codorniz, come here. Listen, you go and ask how to find a church that is about six miles away from here. Go and steal a priest's robes."

"What's the idea?" asked Anastasio in surprise.

"Well, I'll soon find out if this *curro* came here to murder me. I'll tell him he's to be shot. Codorniz will put on the priest's robes, and hear his confession. If he's got anything up his sleeve, I'll shoot him. Otherwise I'll let him go."

"God, there's a roundabout way to tackle the question. I'd just shoot him and let it go at that," said Pancracio contemptuously.

That night Codorniz returned with the priest's robes. Demetrio ordered the prisoner to be led in.

Luis Cervantes, who had not eaten or slept for two days, entered with his face haggard and dark circles under his eyes, his lips dry and colorless.

He spoke awkwardly, slowly:

"You can do as you please with me. . . . I'm convinced I was wrong to come looking for you."

There was a prolonged silence. Then:

"I thought you would welcome a man who comes to offer his help with open arms. Small though my help may be, it's all to your benefit. What, in heaven's name, do I stand to gain, whether the revolution wins or loses?"

Little by little he grew more animated; at times the languor in his eyes disappeared.

"The revolution benefits the poor, the ignorant, all those who have been slaves all their lives, all the unfortunate people who don't even suspect they're poor because the rich take their sweat and blood and tears and turn it into gold. . . ."

"Well, what the hell is this all about? I'll be damned if I can stomach a sermon," Pancracio broke in.

"I wanted to fight for the sacred cause of the oppressed, but you don't understand me . . . you cast me aside. . . . Very well, then, you can do as you please with me!"

"All I'm going to do now is to put this rope around your neck. Look what a pretty white neck you've got."

"Yes, I know what brought you here," Demetrio interrupted dryly, scratching his head. "I'm going to have you shot!"

Then, turning to Anastasio:

"Take him away. And . . . if he wants to confess, bring the priest to him. . . ."

Impassive as ever, Anastasio took Cervantes gently by the arm.

"Come along this way, Curro."

They all laughed uproariously when, a few minutes later, Codorniz appeared in priestly robes.

"By God, this *curro* certainly talks his head off," Codorniz said. "You know, I've a notion he was having a bit of a laugh on me when I started asking him questions."

"But didn't he have anything to confess?"

"Only what he said last night."

"I've a hunch he didn't come here to shoot you at all, compadre," said Anastasio.

"Give him something to eat and keep your eye on him."

VIII

The next day, Luis Cervantes was barely able to get up. His injured leg trailing behind him, he wandered from hut to hut in search of a little alcohol, boiled water, and some rags. With unfailing kindness, Camilla provided him with all that he wanted.

As he began washing his foot, she sat beside him, with the typical curiosity of mountainfolk.

"Tell me, who learned you how to cure people? Why did you boil that water? Why did you boil the rags? . . . Look, look, how careful you are about everything! And what did you put on your hands? Alcohol, really? I just thought liquor was good for a belly-ache, but . . . Oh, I see! So you was going to be a doctor, huh? Ha, ha, that's a good one! Why don't you mix it with cold water! Oh, stop fooling me . . . the idea: little animals alive in the water unless you boil it! Ugh! Well, I can't see nothing in it myself."

Camilla continued to question him with such familiarity that she suddenly found herself addressing him quite informally.

Absorbed in his own thoughts, Luis Cervantes wasn't even listening to her.

Where are those men on Pancho Villa's payroll, so admirably equipped and mounted, who get paid in only pure silver pieces that Villa coins at the Chi-

huahua mint? Bah! Barely two dozen half-naked mangy men, some of them riding decrepit mares with sores from withers to tail. Could what the government press and he himself had stated be true, that these so-called revolutionaries simply are bandits, using the revolution as a wonderful pretext to glut their thirst for gold and blood? Could everything that their sympathizers said about the revolution be a lie?

But if, on the one hand, the newspapers were still proclaiming up and down one government victory after another; on the other hand, a paymaster, recently arrived from Guadalajara, had started the rumor that President Huerta's friends and relatives were abandoning the capital and scurrying away to the nearest port, in spite of Huerta's protestations that "I shall have peace, no matter what the cost."[1] Well, it looked as though the revolutionaries, or bandits, call them what you will, were going to depose the government. Tomorrow would belong to them. A man had to be on their side, only on their side.

"No," he said to himself, almost aloud, "I don't think I've made a mistake this time."

"What did you say?" Camilla asked. "I thought the cat got your tongue."

Luis Cervantes frowned and cast a hostile glance at this little, plump monkey with her bronzed complexion, her ivory teeth, and her thick square feet.

"Look here, Curro, you know how to tell stories, don't you?"

Luis made an impatient gesture and moved off without answering her.

Smitten, she followed him with her eyes until his silhouette was lost on the river path. She was so absorbed in thought that she shuddered in nervous surprise when she heard the voice of her neighbor, one-eyed María Antonia, who had been spying from her hut.

"Hey, you there! . . . Give him some love powder. . . . Then he might fall for you."

"That's what you'd do, all right!"

"As if I wanted to. Ugh! I despise a *curro.* . . ."

IX

"Remigia, lend me some eggs. My hen's hatching her eggs today. I have some gentlemen here who want something to eat."

The neighbor woman's eyes widened as she passed from the bright sunlight into the shadowy hut, darker than usual as dense clouds of smoke rose from the fireplace. After a few moments, she began to make out the outline of things and the wounded man's stretcher in one corner, its head touching the sooty, shiny shed.

She squatted down beside Remigia and, glancing furtively toward where Demetrio was resting, asked in a low voice:

"How's he doing, better? . . . That's fine. Look how young he is! . . . But he's still awfully pale. . . . So, the wound's not closed up yet. Well, Remigia, don't you think we'd better try and do something about it?"

Remigia, naked from the waist up, stretches her thin, sinewy arms over the grinding stone, pounding the corn for the tortillas.

"Oh, I don't know; they might not like it," she answers breathlessly, but without interrupting her work. "They've got their own doctor, you know, so . . ."

"Remigia," another neighbor says as she comes in, bowing her bony back to make it through the door, "don't you have any bay leaves for me to make a potion for María Antonia? She woke up today with a bellyache."

In reality, her errand is just a pretext for asking questions and gossiping, so she turns her eyes to the corner where the patient lies and, winking, asks about his health.

Remigia lowers her eyes to indicate that Demetrio is sleeping....

"Well, then, you're here, too, Pachita? . . . I hadn't noticed you. . . ."

"Good morning to you, Fortunata. How are *you*?"

"All right. But María Antonia's got the curse today and her belly's aching something fierce."

She sits with bent knees, huddling hip to hip against Pachita.

"I've got no bay leaves, honey," Remigia answers, pausing a moment in her work to push a mop of hair back from her sweaty forehead. Then, plunging her two hands into a mass of corn, she grabs a handful of it dripping with murky yellowish water. "I don't have any at all; you'd better go to Dolores, she's always got herbs, you know."

"But Dolores went to her Cofradía[1] last night. I don't know, but they say they came to fetch her to help Uncle Matías's girl deliver her baby."

"You don't say, Pachita?"

The three old women come together, forming an animated group, and, speaking in low tones, begin to gossip excitedly.

"Certainly, I swear it, by God in heaven."

"Well, well, I was the first one to say that Marcelina was getting fat, wasn't I? But, of course, no one would believe me."

"Poor girl.... And worse if it turns out Uncle Nazario's! . . ."

"God help her! . . ."

"Of course it's not her uncle; Nazario had nothing to do with it. It was them damned soldiers, that's who done it."

"Bah! One more poor, unhappy girl."

The cackle of the old hens finally awakened Demetrio.

They kept silent for a moment; then Pachita, taking a nearly smothered, gasping, young pigeon out of her blouse, said:

"To tell you the truth, I brought this medicine for the gentleman here, but they say he's got a doctor, so I suppose . . ."

"That doesn't matter, Pachita . . . , it's just something to rub on his body."

"Forgive this poor gift from a poor woman, señor," said the wrinkled old woman, drawing close to Demetrio, "but there's nothing like it in the world for hemorrhages and suchlike."

Demetrio nodded hasty approval. They had already placed a loaf of bread soaked in alcohol on his stomach; and although when they removed it he began to be cooler, he felt that he was still feverish inside.

"Come on, Remigia, you know how to do it right," the woman exclaimed.

Out of a reed sheath, Remigia pulled a long curved knife that she used to cut cactus fruit. She took the pigeon in one hand, turned it over, its breast upward, and with the skill of a surgeon, cut it in two with a single stroke.

"In the name of Jesus, Mary, and Joseph," Remigia said, making the sign of the cross. Next she quickly placed the warm bleeding portions of the pigeon on Demetrio's abdomen.

"You'll see, you'll feel much better now."

Obeying Remigia's instructions, Demetrio lay curled up on one side without moving.

Then Fortunata gave vent to her sorrows. She liked these gentlemen of the revolution. Three months ago, the Government soldiers had run away with her only daughter, and that had broken her heart, and driven her all but crazy.

At the beginning of her account, Codorniz and Anastasio Montañez, lying at the foot of the stretcher, lifted their heads and listened intently, their mouths agape; but Fortunata went into such minute detail that halfway through the story Codorniz got bored and left the hut to scratch himself out in the sun. By the time Fortunata was finishing with a solemn "I pray God and the Blessed Virgin Mary that you don't spare the life of a single one of those Federals from hell," Demetrio, face to the wall, and feeling greatly relieved by the stomach cure, was busy thinking of the best route by which to proceed to Durango, and Anastasio Montañez was snoring like a trombone.

X

"Why don't you call in the *curro* to treat you, compadre Demetrio?" Anastasio Montañez asked his chief, who had been complaining daily of chills and fever. "You ought to see how he cured himself, and now he's so fit that he doesn't even limp."

But Venancio, standing by with his tins of lard and his dirty rags ready, protested:

"If anybody else lays a hand on Demetrio, I won't be responsible."

"Listen, pal, what kind of doctor do you think you are? I'll wager you've already forgotten why you ever joined us," said Codorniz.

"Yeah, now I remember, Codorniz, that you're with us because you stole a watch and some diamond rings," Venancio replied angrily.

Codorniz burst out laughing.

"That's rich! What's worse? You ran away from your hometown because you poisoned your sweetheart."

"You're a liar!"

"Yes you did! You fed her Spanish fly so that . . ."

Venancio's shout of protest was drowned out in the loud laughter of the others.

Demetrio, with a sour look on his face, motioned for silence. He began to complain and said:

"That'll do. Bring in the student."

Luis Cervantes entered, uncovered Demetrio's leg, examined the wound carefully, and shook his head. The makeshift bandage had made a furrow in the skin; the leg, badly swollen, seemed about to burst. At every move he made, Demetrio stifled a moan. Luis Cervantes cut the ties holding the bandage, thoroughly washed the wound, covered the thigh with large, damp cloths, and bound it up.

Demetrio was able to sleep all afternoon and all night. The next day he woke up happy.

"That *curro* has the gentlest hand in the world!" he said.

Quickly Venancio cut in:

"All right; but don't forget that *curros* are like moisture, they seep in everywhere. It's the *curros* who stopped us reaping the harvest of the revolution."

And since Demetrio believed blindly in the barber's knowledge, when Luis Cervantes came to treat him on the next day, he said:

"Look here, do your best, and as soon as I'm recovered, you can go home or anywhere else you damn well please."

Discreetly, Luis Cervantes made no reply.

A week, then a fortnight, elapsed; the Federal troops seemed to have vanished. On the other hand, there was plenty of corn and beans in the neighboring ranches. The people hated the government so bitterly that they gladly gave assistance to the rebels. Demetrio's men, therefore, were patiently waiting for the complete recovery of their chief.

Day after day, Luis Cervantes remained gloomy and silent.

"By God, I actually believe you're in love, Curro," Demetrio said jokingly one morning, after the daily treatment. He had begun to like him.

Gradually, he began to show an interest in his comfort. He asked him if the soldiers gave him his daily ration of meat and milk. Luis Cervantes was forced to answer that his sole nourishment was whatever the old ranch women happened to give him and that everyone still considered him a stranger or an intruder. "They're all good boys, Curro," Demetrio answered. "You've got to know how to handle them, that's all. You mark my words; starting tomorrow, you won't lack for anything."

In effect, things began to change that very afternoon. Stretched out on the rocky ground, watching the twilight clouds that looked like giant clots of blood, some of Macías's men were listening to Venancio tell amusing episodes from *The Wandering Jew*. Quite a few of them, lulled by the barber's mellifluous voice, began to snore; but Luis Cervantes listened avidly, and as soon as Venancio topped off his talk with some anticlerical comments, he said emphatically:

"Wonderful! You're a most gifted storyteller!"

"Well, I reckon I'm not so bad," Venancio answered, warming to the flattery, "but my parents died and I didn't have a chance to study for a profession."

"That's easy to remedy. Once our cause is victorious, you can easily get a degree. A matter of two or three weeks' assistant's work at some hospital and a letter of recommendation from our chief, Macías, and you'll be a full-fledged doctor. It's like child's play."

From that night onward, Venancio, unlike the others, ceased calling him *curro*. It was Louie, this, and Louie, that, all over the place.

XI

"Look here, Curro, I wanted to tell you something," Camilla called to Luis Cervantes one morning, as he came to the hut for boiling water to treat his foot.

For days the girl had been restless, and her coy ways and her reticence had finally annoyed the man; suddenly stopping, he stood up and, eyeing her squarely, he answered:

"All right. What do you want to tell me?"

Camilla was struck dumb and she couldn't utter a word; her face turned beet red, she shrugged her shoulders and bowed her head to her naked breast. Then, without moving an inch, and staring idiotically at his wound, she said in a whisper:

"Look, how nicely it's healing now! . . . It looks like a red Castille rosebud."

Luis Cervantes frowned with obvious disgust, and he went back to dressing his wound without paying her any more attention.

When he finished, Camilla had vanished.

For three days she was nowhere to be found. It was always her mother, Agapita, who answered Cervantes's call, and boiled the water and the rags for him. He was careful to avoid questioning her. Three days later, Camilla reappeared, more coy and eager than ever.

The more distracted and indifferent Luis Cervantes grew, the bolder Camilla. At last, she said:

"Listen, Curro . . . I want you to go over the words of 'La Adelita'[1] with me, will you? Can't you guess why? . . . So I can sing it over and over again and when you're all gone and you're not here . . . when you're far, far away . . . and you don't even remember me anymore . . ."

To Luis Cervantes, her words were like the noise of a steel knife scraping the side of a flask.

But she didn't notice, and she went on talking, as oblivious as ever:

"Well, I want to tell you something. If you could only see what a wicked man your chief is. . . . Take what happened to me. . . . You know how Demetrio won't let a soul but Mamma cook for him and me take him his food. . . . Well, the other day, I went in with his hot chocolate, and what do you think he did to me, the old fool? He grabs hold of my wrist and he presses it tight, tight as can be, and then he starts pinching my legs. . . . I gave him a good sock. 'Hey, stop it! . . . Quiet down! . . . Stop it, you ill-mannered old man! . . . Let me go . . . let me go, you old fool!' I pulled back, slipped away, and ran out of there as fast as I could. . . . What do you think of that, Curro?"

Camilla had never seen Luis Cervantes laugh so hard.

"But is it really true what you're telling me?"

Utterly at a loss, Camilla could not answer. Then he burst into laughter again and repeated the question. And she, with a sinking feeling, answered him in a weak voice:

"Yes, it's the truth. . . . And that's what I wanted to tell you about. Doesn't it make you mad, Curro?"

Once more, Camilla glanced adoringly at Luis Cervantes's fresh, clean face; at his soft green eyes, his smooth cheeks, pink as a porcelain doll's; at his tender white skin that showed under his collar and below the sleeves of his rough woolen shirt; at his hair, blond and ever so slightly curled.

"What the devil are you waiting for, silly fool? If the chief likes you, what more do you want?"

Camilla felt something rise within her breast, something that tightened like a knot in her throat. She squeezed her eyes shut to hold back the tears that welled up in them; then, with the back of her hand, she wiped her wet cheeks, and just as she had done three days ago, fled with all the swiftness of a young deer.

XII

Demetrio's wound had healed. They began to discuss various projects to go northward where, according to rumor, the rebels had beaten the Federal troops all along the line. A certain incident brought things to a head. Seated on a crag of the sierra in the cool of the afternoon, Luis Cervantes gazed off in the distance, dreaming and killing time. Below the narrow rock, Pancracio and Manteca, lying like lizards between the reeds along the riverbank, were playing cards. Anastasio Montañez, looking on indifferently, turned his black-bearded face and his sweet eyes toward Luis Cervantes and said:

"Why so sad, Curro? What are you daydreaming about? Come on over here and let's have a chat. . . ."

Luis Cervantes did not move; but Anastasio went over and sat down beside him like a friend.

"What you need is the excitement of the city. I wager you shine your shoes every day and wear a necktie. Look, Curro, the way you see me right now, all dirty and ragged, I'm not what I seem to be. . . . You don't believe me? . . . I don't have to be here; I own ten pairs of oxen. Really! . . . Go ask my compadre Demetrio. . . . I have my fifteen acres of land to sow. . . . Don't you believe me? . . . Look,

Curro; I just like to get the Federals mad, and that's why they hate me. The last time, eight months ago (that's how long I've been with these guys), I stuck my knife into some little smart-aleck captain (God help me), right here, right in the belly button. . . . But, really, I don't have to be here. . . . I joined up because of that . . . and to help out my compadre Demetrio. . . ."

"Sweet lady luck!" Manteca shouted, waxing enthusiastic over a winning hand. He placed a twenty-cent silver coin on the jack of spades.

"If you want my opinion, I'm not much on gambling. . . . Do you want to bet? . . . Well, come on then, I'm game. How do you like the sound of this leather snake jingling, eh?" Anastasio shook his belt and made the silver coins ring.

Meanwhile, Pancracio dealt the cards, the jack of spades turned up out of the deck and a quarrel ensued. Quarreling, shouts, and, at last, insults. Pancracio brought his stony face close to Manteca, who looked at him with snake's eyes, convulsive, foaming at the mouth. Another moment and they would have come to blows. Having completely exhausted their most pointed insults, they now resorted to referring to each other's fathers and mothers with richly embroidered indecencies.

Still nothing happened; when they ran out of insults, the game ended, they threw their arms about each other's shoulders, and marched off in search of a good stiff drink.

"I don't like to fight with my tongue either, it's not decent. Right, Curro? . . . Really, look, no one has ever insulted my family. . . . I like to be respected. That's why you never see me fooling with anyone. . . . Listen, Curro," Anastasio continued, changing his tone and standing up with one hand over his eyes. "What's that dust cloud over there behind that little hill? By God, what if it's those damned Federals, and us sitting here doing nothing. Come on, let's go and warn the rest of the boys."

———

The news was met with cries of joy.

"Ah, we're going to meet them!" Pancracio was the first to say.

"Yes, we're going to meet them! We'll strip them clean of everything they brought with them...."

But the enemy turned out to be a few burros and two mule drivers.

"Stop them, anyhow. They're from the highlands and they've probably got news for us," Demetrio said.

Indeed, their news proved sensational. The Federal troops had fortified the hills of El Grillo and La Bufa in Zacatecas; this was said to be Huerta's last stronghold, and everybody predicted the fall of the city. Many families were hastily fleeing southward; trains were overloaded with people; there was a scarcity of trucks and coaches; hundreds of people, panic-stricken, walked along the highway with their belongings on their backs. General Pánfilo Natera[1] was assembling his men at Fresnillo; the Federals already felt it was all over for them.

"The fall of Zacatecas will be Huerta's *Requiescat in pace*," Luis Cervantes stated with unusual vehemence. "We've got to be there before the fight starts so that we can join Natera's army."

And noting the looks of surprise on the faces of Demetrio and his men, he realized they still considered him to be of no account.

But the next day, as the men set off in search of good mounts before taking to the road again, Demetrio called Luis Cervantes:

"Do you really want to come with us, Curro? Of course, you're cut from another timber, we all know that; I don't understand why you should like this sort of life.... Do you imagine we're in this game because we like it? Now, I like the excitement all right, but that's not all.... Sit down, Curro, sit down, and I'll tell you my story. Do you know why I'm a rebel?... Look, before the revolution, I had my land all plowed and ready for sowing, and if it hadn't been for a little quarrel with Don Mónico, the boss of my town, Moyahua, I'd be there hurrying to get the oxen ready for planting.... Pancracio, pull down two bottles of beer for me and Curro.... By the Holy Cross ... drinking won't hurt me, now, will it?"

XIII

"I was born in Limón, close by Moyahua, right in the heart of the Juchipila canyon. I had my house and my cows and a patch of land: I had everything I needed. Well, mister, we farmers make a habit of going over to town every week. You hear mass and the sermon, and then you go to market to buy your onions and tomatoes and everything else. Then you pick up some friends and go to Primitivo López's saloon for a bite of lunch. You have a drink; you've got to be sociable, so you drink more than you should, and the liquor goes to your head and you laugh and you're damned happy, and if you feel like it, you sing and shout and carry on. That's quite all right, because we're not doing anyone any harm. But if they start bothering you, and if the policeman walks up and down and stops to put his ear to the door, and if the chief of police and his gang decide to put a stop to your fun . . . Sure, man, you've got red blood in your veins and a soul, too, and you lose your temper, you stand up to them and tell them to go to the Devil. Now, if they understand you, everything's all right; they leave you alone, and that's all there is to it. But sometimes they try to talk you down . . . well, you know how it is, a fellow's quick tempered and he'll be damned if he'll stand for someone ordering him around. . . . So, before you know it, you've got your knife out or your gun; and then off you go to the sierra, until they forget about the dead man.

"All right. What happened with Don Mónico? Nothing compared to the others. Smart aleck! He couldn't tell a rooster from a hen. Well, I spit on his beard because he wouldn't mind his own business. That's all, there's nothing else to tell. But that was enough for him to send the whole goddamned Federal Government against me. You must have heard something about the goings-on in Mexico City, where they killed Madero and some other fellow, Félix or Felipe Díaz,[1] I don't know! . . . Well, this Don Mónico went in person to Zacatecas to bring a posse to capture me. They said that I was a Maderista and that I was going to rebel. But a man like me always has friends. Somebody came and warned me just in time, so when the Federals reached Limón, I was miles and miles away. Then my compadre Anastasio, who killed somebody, came and joined me, and Pancracio and Codorniz and a lot of friends and acquaintances. Since then others have been joining us. You know for yourself, we get along as best we can. . . ."

For a few moments, both men sat meditating in silence.

"Chief," said Luis Cervantes. "You know that some of Natera's men are at Juchipila, quite near here. I think we should join them before they capture Zacatecas. All we need do is speak to the General."

"I'm no good at that sort of thing. . . . And I don't like the idea of accepting orders from anybody."

"But you've only a handful of men down here; you'll only be an unimportant chieftain. The revolution is bound to win; after it's all over, they'll talk to you just as Madero talked to all those who had helped him: 'Thank you very much, my friends, you can go home now.' . . ."

"Well, that's all I want, to be left alone so I can go home."

"Wait a moment, I haven't finished. Madero said: 'You men have made me President of the Republic; risking your lives and leaving your widows and orphaned children destitute; now that I have what I wanted, you can go back to your picks and shovels, you can resume your hand-to-mouth existence, always hungry and naked just as you were before, while we, your superiors, will go about trying to pile up a few million pesos. . . .' "

Demetrio nodded and, smiling, scratched his head.

"You said a mouthful, Louie," Venancio, the barber, put in enthusiastically.

"As I was saying," Luis Cervantes resumed, "when the revolution is over, everything is over. Too bad that so many men have been killed, too bad there are so many widows and orphans, too bad there was so much bloodshed. And what for? So a few rascals can get rich and everything else stays the same as before or maybe even gets worse? Of course, you're not selfish; you say to yourself: 'All I want to do is go back home.' But I ask you, is it fair to deprive your wife and kids of a fortune which God himself places within reach of your hand? Is it fair to abandon your motherland in this solemn moment when she most needs the self-sacrifice of her humble sons to save her from falling again into the clutches of her eternal oppressors, executioners, and *caciques*? You must not forget that the thing a man holds most sacred on earth is his family and his homeland."

Macías smiled, his eyes shining.

"Will it be all right if we go with Natera, Curro?"

"Not only all right," Venancio said insinuatingly, "but I think it absolutely necessary."

"Chief," Cervantes pursued, "I took a fancy to you the first time I laid eyes on you, and I like you more and more every day, because I realize what you are worth. Please let me be utterly frank. You still don't realize your true, lofty, noble mission. You are a modest man without ambitions, you do not wish to realize the exceedingly important role you are destined to play in the revolution. It's not true that you took up arms simply because of Don Mónico, the *cacique*. You rose up to protest against the evils of all the *caciques* who are ruining the whole nation. We are elements of a great social movement that will not rest until it has enlarged the destinies of our motherland. We are the tools Destiny makes use of to reclaim the sacred rights of the people. We are not fighting to dethrone a miserable murderer; we are fighting against tyranny itself. That's what it means to fight for principles, to defend ideals. That's why Villa and Natera and Carranza[2] are fighting; that's why we, every man of us, are fighting."

"Yes . . . yes . . . exactly what I've been thinking myself," said Venancio in a climax of enthusiasm.

"Hey, there, Pancracio," Macías called, "pull down two more beers."

XIV

"You ought to see how clear that fellow can make things, compadre," Demetrio said, pondering as much of Luis Cervantes's speech as he had understood that morning.

"I heard him, too," Anastasio answered. "People who can read and write get things clear, all right. But what I can't make out is how you're going to go and meet Natera with as few men as we have."

"That's nothing. We're going to do things differently now. They tell me that as soon as Crispín Robles enters a town he gets hold of all the horses and guns he can find; then he goes to the jail and lets all the prisoners out, and, before you know it, he's got plenty of men. You'll see. You know, I'm beginning to feel that we haven't done things right so far. It doesn't seem right somehow that this city guy should be able to tell us what to do."

"Ain't it wonderful to be able to read and write!"

They both sighed, sadly.

Luis Cervantes came in with several others to find out the day of their departure.

"We're leaving tomorrow," said Demetrio without hesitation.

Codorniz suggested bringing musicians from the neighboring

hamlet and having a farewell dance. His idea met with enthusiasm from all sides.

"Let's go, then," Pancracio shouted, "but I'm going in good company this time. My sweetheart's coming along with me!"

Demetrio replied that he, too, would willingly take along a girl he had set his eye on, but that he hoped none of his men would leave bitter memories behind them as the Federals did.

"You won't have long to wait. Everything will be arranged when you return," Luis Cervantes said, in a low voice.

"What do you mean?" Demetrio asked. "I thought that you and Camilla . . . "

"There's not of word of truth in it, chief. She likes you . . . but she's afraid of you."

"Really, Curro?"

"Yes. But I think you're quite right about not wanting to leave any bitter feelings behind. When we come back in triumph, everything will be different. They'll all thank you for it, even."

"By God, you're certainly a shrewd one," Demetrio replied, smiling and patting him on the back.

At sundown, Camilla went to the river to fetch water, as usual. Luis Cervantes, walking down the same trail, met her.

Camilla felt her heart leap to her mouth.

Perhaps without taking the slightest notice of her, Luis Cervantes hastily disappeared among the rocks.

At that hour, like every day, shadows softened the tones of the calcinated rocks, the sunburned branches, and the dry weeds. The wind blew softly, rocking the green lances of the young corn. Everything was the same as always; but in the stones and the dry branches, in the fragrant air and the swirling leaves, Camilla sensed something strange, as if there were a vast desolation in everything around her.

Rounding a huge eroded rock, suddenly Camilla found herself face to face with Luis, who was seated on a boulder, hatless, his legs dangling.

"Hey, Curro, come say good-bye to me at least."

Luis Cervantes was obliging enough; he jumped down and came over to her.

"You're proud, ain't you? Did I take such poor care of you that you don't even want to talk to me?"

"Why do you say that, Camilla? You've been very good to me; why, you've been more than a friend, you've taken care of me like a sister. I'm very grateful to you; and I'll always remember what you did."

"Liar!" Camilla said, her face transfigured with joy. "Suppose I hadn't spoken to you?"

"I was going to thank you at the dance this evening."

"What dance? . . . Even if there's a dance, I won't go."

"Why not?"

"Because I can't stand that horrible man . . . Demetrio!"

"How foolish! . . . Look, he's really very fond of you. Don't miss your chance, it won't come again. Silly girl, Demetrio is on the verge of becoming a general, a rich man. . . . Horses galore, jewels and fine clothes, fancy houses and a lot of money to spend. Just imagine what a life you would lead with him!"

Camilla stared up at the blue sky so that he wouldn't see her eyes. A dead leaf shook loose from the crest of a tree and, swinging slowly on the wind, fell like a small dead butterfly at her feet. She bent down and took it in her fingers. Then, without looking at him, she murmured:

"Oh, Curro . . . if you only knew how bad I feel when you talk like that. . . . It's you I like . . . just you. . . . Go away, Curro, get out of here. I don't know why I feel so ashamed. . . . Go away!"

She threw away the leaf she had crumpled with her anguished fingers and covered her face with a corner of her apron.

When she opened her eyes, Luis Cervantes had disappeared.

She followed the path along the stream. The water seemed to have been sprinkled with a fine red dust; on its waves played the reflection of the colors of the sky and of the dark crags, half light, and half shadow. Myriads of luminous insects twinkled in a hollow. And, in the pebbled depths of the stream, she appeared in her yellow blouse with the green ribbons, her white skirt; her carefully combed hair, her wide eyebrows and broad forehead; exactly as she had dressed to please Luis.

She burst into tears.

Among the reeds, the frogs chanted the implacable melancholy of the hour.

Swaying on a dry tree limb, a dove wept also.

XV

At the dance, there was much merrymaking, and they drank a good mezcal.

"I miss Camilla," said Demetrio in a loud voice.

Everybody looked about for Camilla.

"She's sick, she's got a headache," said Agapita harshly, annoyed by the malicious glances leveled at her.

When the dance was over, Demetrio, somewhat unsteady on his feet, thanked all the kind neighbors who had welcomed them and promised that when the revolution triumphed he would remember them one and all, because "hospital or jail is a true test of friendship."

"May God's hand keep you safe," said an old woman.

"God bless you all and guide you," others added.

Utterly drunk, María Antonia said:

"Come back soon, damn soon!"

The next day, María Antonia, who, though she was pockmarked and walleyed, nevertheless enjoyed a notorious reputation—so notorious that it was said there wasn't a man around who hadn't enjoyed her company—shouted to Camilla:

"Hey there, you! . . . What's the matter? . . . What are you doing there skulking in the corner with a shawl tied round your head! You're crying? Look at her eyes! You look like a witch! There's no sorrow lasts more than three days!"

Agapita frowned and muttered indistinctly to herself.

The old crones felt uneasy and lonesome since Demetrio's men had left, and even the men, in spite of the gossip and insults, lamented that there was no one left to provide the ranch with sheep and calves for fresh meat every day. It is pleasant, indeed, to spend your time eating, and drinking, and sleeping all day long in the cool shade of the rocks, while clouds form and dissolve in the sky.

"Look at them again! There they go!" María Antonia yelled. "They look like figurines."

Far off, where the brambles and the chaparral began to melt into one velvety blue surface, Demetrio Macías's men, riding their thin nags along the crest of a hill, were silhouetted against the bright sapphire sky. A gust of hot wind carried the faint, faltering strains of "La Adelita" to the settlement.

Camilla, who had come out to see them one last time when María Antonia shouted, could no longer control herself, and she went back inside, overcome with sobbing.

María Antonia burst into laughter and moved off.

"They've cast the evil eye on my daughter," Agapita mumbled in perplexity.

She pondered a while, then reached a decision: from a pole in the hut that stood between a picture of Christ and one of the Virgin of Jalpa, she took down a piece of strong leather that her husband used to hitch up the yoke. Agapita doubled the leather strap and gave Camilla a sound thrashing to dispel the evil spirits.

———

Riding on his chestnut horse, Demetrio felt like a new man. His eyes recovered their peculiar, metallic brilliance, and the blood flowed, red and warm, through the coppery cheeks of his indigenous race.

The men threw out their chests as if to breathe the widening horizon, the immensity of the sky, the blue of the mountains, and the fresh air, scented with the aromas of the sierra. They spurred their horses to a gallop as if in that mad race they laid claim to the whole earth. What man among them now remembered the stern chief of police, the growling policeman, or the conceited *cacique*? What man remembered his pitiful hut where he slaved away, always under the eyes of the owner or the ruthless and sullen foreman, always forced to rise before dawn and to take up his shovel and basket, or the plow and goad, only to earn the daily pitcher of *atole*[1] and a handful of beans?

They sang, they laughed, they whistled, drunk with the sunlight, the air, and life itself.

Meco, prancing forward on his horse, bared his white teeth, joking and clowning around.

"Hey, Pancracio," he asked with utmost seriousness, "my wife writes me I've got another kid. How in hell is that? I ain't seen her since Madero was President."

"That's nothing. You just left her with eggs to hatch!"

They all laugh uproariously. Only Meco, grave and aloof, sings in a horrible falsetto:

> "A penny I gave her,
> And she said no.
> I gave her a nickel
> That she still refused.
> She begged me so hard
> I gave her two bits.
> Oh, how ungrateful women are!"

The racket ended as the sun dulled their senses.

All day long they rode through the canyon, up and down the steep, round hills, bald and dirty as a scabby scalp, hill after hill in endless succession.

Late in the afternoon, several small stone towers appeared far off in the heart of a bluish ridge, and, beyond, the road with its curling spirals of dust and its gray telegraph poles.

They advanced toward the main road; and in the distance they spied the figure of a man squatting on the side of the road. They drew up to him. He proved to be an unfriendly-looking old man, clad in rags. He was laboriously attempting to mend his leather sandals with the help of a dull knife. A burro loaded with fresh green grass stood close by.

Demetrio asked:

"What are you doing, Grandpa?"

"I'm heading to town with alfalfa for my cow."

"How many Federals are there around here?"

"Just a few; not even a dozen, I reckon."

The old man grew more communicative. He said that there were many serious rumors going around: Obregón was besieging Guadalajara, Carrera Torres[2] was in control of San Luis Potosí, and Pánfilo Natera ruled over Fresnillo.

"All right," said Demetrio, "you can go off to your own town, but you be careful not to tell anyone you saw us, because if you do, I'll pump you full of lead. And I could track you down, even if you tried to hide in the center of the earth."

"What do you say, boys?" Demetrio asked them as soon as the old man had moved off.

"To hell with the *mochos*! We'll kill every blasted one of them!" they cried in unison.

Then they set to counting their cartridges and the hand grenades that Tecolote[3] had made out of fragments of iron tubing and metal bed handles.

"Not much to brag about, but we'll soon trade them for rifles," Anastasio observed.

Anxiously they pressed forward, spurring the thin flanks of their exhausted nags to a gallop.

Demetrio's imperious voice brought them abruptly to a halt.

They camped by the side of a hill, protected by thick huisache trees. Without unsaddling their horses, they each began to search for a stone to serve as a pillow.

XVI

At midnight Demetrio Macías ordered the march to be resumed.

The town was five or six miles away; and they had to make a predawn attack on the soldiers. The sky was cloudy, here and there a star twinkled, and from time to time the far horizon was illuminated by a red flash of lightning.

Luis Cervantes asked Demetrio if it wouldn't be a good idea, for the success of the attack, to have a guide, or at least to obtain the topographic conditions of the town and the precise location of the soldiers' quarters.

"No, Curro," Demetrio answered, accompanying his smile with a disdainful gesture. "We'll simply fall on them when they least expect it; that's all there is to it. We've done it that way lots of times. Haven't you ever seen the ground squirrels stick their heads out of their holes when you fill them up with water? Well, these lousy soldiers are going to be just as stunned as that, the moment they hear the first shots. When they come out, it'll be like target practice."

"What if the old man we met yesterday lied to us? Suppose there are fifty soldiers instead of twenty. What if he's a spy sent out by the Federals!"

"Ha, Curro, frightened already!" Anastasio Montañez said.

"Sure! Messing about with bandages and handling a rifle are two different things," Pancracio observed.

"Well, that's enough talk, I guess," said Meco. "All we have to do is fight a dozen frightened rats."

"This fight won't convince our mothers that they gave birth to real men. . . . " Manteca added.

When they reached the outskirts of the town, Venancio walked ahead and knocked at the door of a hut.

"Where's the barracks?" he asked the man who came out barefoot, a ragged serape covering his bare chest.

"The barracks is just below the plaza, boss," he answered.

But since nobody knew where the plaza was, Venancio made him walk ahead to show the way.

Trembling with fear, the poor devil told them they were doing him a terrible wrong. "I'm just a poor day laborer, señor; I've got a wife and a lot of kids."

"What the hell do you think I have, dogs?" Demetrio scowled. Then he commanded:

"You men keep quiet, and walk down the middle of the street, single file."

The rectangular church cupola rose above the small houses.

"Look, gentlemen; there's the plaza in front of the church; walk a bit farther down and there's the barracks."

Then he knelt down, imploring them to let him go home, but Pancracio, without replying, struck him across the chest with his rifle and ordered him to proceed.

"How many soldiers are there?" Luis Cervantes asked.

"I don't want to lie to you, boss, but to tell you the truth, yes, señor, to tell you God's truth, there's a lot of them."

Luis Cervantes turned around to stare at Demetrio, who pretended he hadn't heard.

They were soon in a small plaza.

A loud volley of rifle shots deafened them. Demetrio's chestnut horse staggered, bent its forelegs, and fell to the ground, kicking. Tecolote uttered a piercing cry and tumbled off his horse, which rushed madly to the center of the square.

Another volley, and the guide threw up his arms and fell on his back without a sound.

Anastasio Montañez quickly helped Demetrio up behind him on his horse. The others had already retreated and were seeking shelter along the walls of the houses.

"Hey, men," said a townsman sticking his head out of a large doorway, "go for 'em through the back of the chapel. They're all in there. Cut back through this street, then turn to the left; then you'll reach an alley and keep on going straight ahead until you hit the chapel."

At that moment a fresh volley of pistol shots, coming from the neighboring roofs, fell like rain about them.

"Huh," the man said, "those ain't poisonous spiders. . . . It's the new recruits. . . . Come in here until they stop. . . . "

"How many of them are there?" asked Demetrio.

"There were only twelve of them here, but last night they were scared out of their wits so they wired to the next town for help. Who knows how many there are? But it doesn't matter anyhow. Most of them are draftees; if just one of them turns tail, they'll all desert. My brother was drafted; they've got him in there, the bastards. I'll go along with you and signal to him; and you'll see how they'll all come over to your side. Then we'll only have the officers to deal with! But if you want to give me a gun or something . . . "

"No more rifles left, brother. But I guess you can put these to some use," Anastasio Montañez said, passing him two hand grenades.

The officer in command of the Federals was a conceited young captain with a waxed mustache and blond hair. As long as he was unsure about the strength of the assailants, he had remained extremely quiet and prudent; but now that they had driven the rebels back without allowing them a chance to fire a single shot, he made much of his singular courage and boldness. While his soldiers hardly dared to poke their heads up from behind the portico walls, he displayed his slender silhouette and billowing cape against the pale light of dawn.

"Ha, I remember our coup d'état!"

Since his military career consisted of the single adventure when, together with other students of the Officers' School, he was involved in the treacherous revolt against President Madero, whenever the slightest motive arose, he invariably recalled his feat at the Ciudadela.[1]

"Lieutenant Campos," he ordered emphatically, "go down with ten men and wipe out the bandits hiding there! . . . The curs! They're only brave when it comes to gobbling meat and stealing chickens!"

A civilian appeared at the small door of the spiral staircase, announcing that the assailants were hidden in a corral where they might easily be captured.

This message came from the prominent citizens of the town who were posted on the housetops, alert against the enemies' escape.

"I'll go myself and get it over with!" the officer declared impetuously. But he soon changed his mind. At the staircase door, he retraced his steps.

"Very likely they are waiting for more men, and it would be wrong for me to abandon my post. Lieutenant Campos, go there yourself and capture them all alive so we can shoot them at noon when everybody's coming out of church. Those bandits will see the example I'll set around here. But if you can't capture them, Lieutenant, kill them all. Don't leave a single one of them alive, do you understand?"

In high good humor, he began pacing up and down the room, thinking over the official report he would send off no later than today.

To His Honor the Minister for War
General Aureliano Blanquet
Mexico City

Sir:

I have the honor to inform your Excellency that on the morning of . . . a rebel army, five hundred strong, commanded by . . . dared to attack this town. With such speed as the gravity of the situation called for, I fortified my post in the high grounds of the settlement. The battle began at dawn and lasted for two hours of heavy gunfire. Despite the superiority of the enemy in men and equipment, I was able to defeat and rout them. Their casualties were twenty killed and a far greater number wounded, judging from the trails of blood they left behind in their hasty retreat. I am pleased to state that there was no casualty on our side. I have the honor to congratulate your Excellency upon this new triumph for the Federal forces. Viva Presidente Huerta! Viva Mexico!

"And then," the young captain mused, "my promotion to major is assured." He clasped his hands together jubilantly, at the very moment that an explosion left his ears buzzing.

XVII

"If we get through the corral, we can make the alley, eh?" Demetrio asked.

"That's right," the townsman answered. "Beyond the corral there's a house, then another corral, then a store beyond that."

Demetrio scratched his head, thoughtfully. But his decision was immediate.

"Can you get hold of a crowbar or a pick or something like that to make a hole through the wall?"

"Yes, we have everything, but . . ."

"But what? Where are they?"

"Everything is right there; but it all belongs to the boss and . . ."

Demetrio, without listening to the rest, strode into the shed that had been pointed out as the toolhouse.

It was all a matter of a few minutes.

Once in the alley, hugging the walls, they ran ahead one by one until they reached the rear of the church.

First they had to scale an adobe wall, then the rear wall of the chapel.

"God's will be done!" Demetrio thought. He was the first to clamber over.

Like monkeys, the others followed him, reaching the top with bleeding, grimy hands. The rest was easier: deep worn steps along the stonework let them clear the chapel wall easily; then the dome itself hid them from the soldiers.

"Wait a moment," said the man. "I'll go and see where my brother is. I'll give the signal . . . and then you'll get at the officers."

But no one paid the slightest attention to him.

For a second, Demetrio studied the dark stain of the army capes along the stone wall, across the front and down the sides, in the towers crowded with people, behind the iron railing.

He smiled with satisfaction, and, turning to his men, exclaimed: "Now! . . ."

Twenty bombs exploded simultaneously in the midst of the soldiers, who, terrified, started up, their eyes wide open. But before they had fully understood their plight, twenty more bombs burst like thunder upon them, leaving a stream of men killed and maimed.

"Not yet! . . . Not yet! . . . I still don't see my brother," the civilian implored.

In vain, an old sergeant harangues the soldiers and insults them in hopes of rallying them to their own defense. They're nothing more than rats caught in a trap. Some try to reach the door by the staircase, and fall to the ground, pierced by Demetrio's shots. Others fall at the feet of those twenty-odd specters, with faces and breasts dark as iron, and long, torn trousers of white cloth, which hang to their leather sandals. In the belfry, a few men struggle to emerge from the pile of dead who have fallen upon them.

"Chief!" Luis Cervantes cries in alarm. "We're out of bombs and our guns are in the corral. Now what? . . ."

Smiling, Demetrio draws out a large shining knife. Instantly, steel flashes in twenty hands, some large and pointed, others wide as the palm of a hand, heavy as bayonets.

"The spy!" Luis Cervantes shouts triumphantly. "Didn't I tell you?"

"Don't kill me, Chief," the old sergeant implores at the feet of Demetrio, who stands over him, knife in hand.

The old man raises his face with its indigenous features full of wrinkles but without a single gray hair. Demetrio recognizes the spy who had lied to him the day before.

Terrified, Luis Cervantes quickly averts his face. The steel blade stumbles on his ribs, *crack crack*, and the old man topples backward, his arms spread and his eyes open in a ghostly stare.

"Not my brother, no! . . . Don't kill him, he's my brother!" the civilian shouts in terror to Pancracio, who is pursuing a Federal.

It's too late. With one thrust, Pancracio has sliced his neck open, and two streams of scarlet spurt like a fountain.

Pancracio and Manteca surpass the others in the butchery by killing off the wounded. Montañez, exhausted, lets his hand fall limp; he still has that sweet look in his eyes; a child's naïveté and a jackal's amorality light up his face.

"Here's one who's not dead yet," Codorniz shouts.

Pancracio runs toward him. It's the little blond captain with the curled mustache, pale as wax, leaning in a corner near the staircase and unable to muster enough strength to take another step.

Pancracio pushes him brutally to the edge of the wall. A jab with his knee against that captain's hip, and then something like a sack of stones falling twenty yards down onto the porch of the church.

"My God, you've got no brains!" shouts Codorniz. "If I'd suspected you'd do that, I wouldn't have told you. That was a fine pair of shoes that I was going to take!"

The men, bending over now, strip the best-clad soldiers, laughing and joking as they put on their booty.

Brushing back the long hair that has fallen over his sweaty forehead and covers his eyes, Demetrio says:

"Now let's get those city fellows!"

XVIII

Demetrio arrived in Fresnillo with one hundred men the same day that General Pánfilo Natera began his advance against the town of Zacatecas.

The leader from Zacatecas received him cordially.

"I know who you are and the sort of men you bring! I heard about the beatings you've given the Federals from Tepic to Durango."

Natera shook hands with Macías effusively, while Luis Cervantes bragged:

"With men like General Natera and Colonel Macías, we'll cover our country with glory."

Demetrio understood the purpose of those words, after Natera had repeatedly addressed him as "Colonel."

Wine and beer were served. Demetrio and Natera drank many a toast. Luis Cervantes proposed a toast to "the triumph of our cause, which is the sublime triumph of Justice; for our ideals—to free the noble, long-suffering people of Mexico—to be quickly realized, and for those men who have watered the earth with their blood to reap the harvest which is rightfully theirs."

Natera fixed his stern gaze on the orator, then turned his back on him to talk to Demetrio.

Presently, one of Natera's officers drew up to the table and stared insistently at Cervantes. He was a young man with a frank, cordial face.

"Luis Cervantes? ... "

"Solís?"

"The moment you entered I thought I recognized you.... Well, well, even now I can hardly believe my eyes!"

"It's true enough!"

"Well, but ... look here, let's have a drink, come along."

"Hm," Solís went on, offering Cervantes a chair, "since when have you turned rebel?"

"The last two months!"

"Oh, I see! That's why you still speak with that faith and that enthusiasm we all had at the beginning!"

"Have you lost it then?"

"Look here, man, don't be surprised if I confide in you right off. I'm so anxious to find someone intelligent to talk to, that as soon as I get hold of a man like you I clutch at him as eagerly as a glass of water, after walking mile after mile under the blazing sun.... But honestly, first I want you to explain.... I can't understand how a correspondent for a Government newspaper during Madero's time, who wrote furious articles in *El Regional*, who denounced us as bandits, is now fighting on our side."

"I tell you honestly, I have been converted," Cervantes answered emphatically.

"You, converted?"

Solís sighed; he filled their glasses, and they drank.

"Are you tired of the revolution then?" asked Cervantes evasively.

"Tired? ... I'm twenty-five years old and I'm fit as a fiddle! ... But am I disappointed? Perhaps!"

"You must have your reasons...."

"I'd hoped to find a meadow at the end of the road ... and I found a swamp. My friend, there are facts and there are men that are pure poison. . . . And that poison drips into your soul and turns everything bitter. Enthusiasm, hopes, ideals, joys . . . all come to naught. . . . Then you have no other choice: either you turn into a bandit just like them; or you disappear, hiding behind a mask of the most ferocious and impenetrable egotism."

The conversation was like torture for Luis Cervantes; it was a painful sacrifice for him to hear such unexpected words. To avoid having to take part in it, he invited Solís to tell him in detail what circumstances had led him to such a state of disillusionment.

"Circumstances? It's a host of silly, insignificant things: gestures that no one notices except yourself; a change of expression, eyes shining . . . lips curled in a sneer; the fleeting meaning of a phrase that is lost! But they are deeds, gestures, and expressions that taken together constitute the frightful and grotesque grimace of a whole race. . . . A race without redemption! . . . " He drained another glass of wine, took a long pause and continued: "You may ask me why I stay with the revolution. Well, the revolution is like the hurricane, and the man who joins it isn't a man anymore . . . he's a miserable dead leaf caught up in the windstorm."

Solís was interrupted by Demetrio Macías, who approached them.

"Come along, Curro."

Alberto Solís, speaking with a facile tongue and deeply sincere tones, congratulated him effusively on the feats and adventures that had made him famous and had even won him recognition among the men of the powerful Northern Division.

And Demetrio, charmed by his praise, listened to the story of his own deeds so well composed and arranged that he hardly recognized them. But it sounded so good that before long he found himself repeating it in the same way, and believing it, too.

"What a fine man Natera is!" Luis Cervantes said when they returned to the hotel. "Captain Solís, on the other hand, is a nuisance."

Demetrio Macías, too elated to listen to him, took his arm and said in a low voice:

"I'm a colonel, Curro. . . . And you're my secretary!"

Macías's men made many acquaintances that evening; much liquor flowed to celebrate new friendships. Of course, not everyone gets along, nor is alcohol a good counselor; quarrels naturally ensued. But everything was smoothed out in a friendly spirit, outside the saloons, restaurants, or brothels, without bothering anyone.

The next morning, a few people woke up dead: an old prostitute, with a bullet through her stomach; two of Colonel Macías's new recruits, with their skulls cracked open. Anastasio Montañez carried an account of the events to his chief, who shrugged his shoulders, saying "Psh! . . . Go ahead and bury them. . . . "

XIX

"They're coming back!" the inhabitants of Fresnillo exclaimed with amazement when they learned that the rebel attack on Zacatecas had failed completely.

The rebels were a maddened mob, sunburnt, filthy, naked. Their high, wide-brimmed straw hats hid their faces.

The "high hats," as they were called, came back as happily as when they had marched away a few days before, pillaging every hamlet along the road, every ranch, even the poorest hut.

"Who'll buy this thing?" one of them asked, red faced and tired from carrying his spoils.

It was a brand-new typewriter, and the shiny nickel-plate attracted everyone's eye.

Five times that morning the Oliver had changed hands. The first sale netted ten pesos; presently it had sold for eight; each time it changed hands, it was two pesos cheaper. To be sure, it was a heavy burden; nobody could carry it for more than a half hour.

"I'll give you a quarter for it!" Codorniz offered.

"Yours!" cried the owner, handing it over quickly, as though he feared he might change his mind.

Thus, for the sum of twenty-five cents, Codorniz was afforded the pleasure of taking it in his hands and throwing it against the rocks, smashing it to pieces.

This gave the signal: everyone who was burdened with cumbersome objects began to unload them, shattering them on the rocks. Crystal and china, heavy mirrors, brass candlesticks, delicate statues, jugs, and all the useless spoils flew through the air and broke into a thousand pieces.

Demetrio, who did not share the untoward exaltation in light of the results of the military operation, called Montañez and Pancracio aside and said:

"These fellows have no guts. It's not so hard to take a town. It's like this. First, you open up, this way . . . then you come closer and closer together until, bang! . . . And that's it!"

And with a broad gesture he opened his powerful arms, then brought them slowly back together, gesturing as he spoke until he pressed his arms against his chest in a viselike grip.

Anastasio and Pancracio, convinced by this simple, lucid explanation answered:

"That's God's truth! They've got no guts!"

Demetrio's men camped in a corral.

"Do you remember Camilla, compadre Anastasio?" Demetrio asked with a sigh as he settled on his back on the manure pile where the rest were already stretched out.

"Camilla who, compadre?"

"The girl who used to feed me up there at the ranch!"

Anastasio made a gesture implying, "I don't care a damn about women."

"I can't forget her," Demetrio went on, drawing on his cigarette. "I was feeling like hell! I'd just finished drinking a glass of fresh water. God, but it was cool. . . . 'Don't you want any more?' she asked me. I was half dead with fever . . . and all I saw was that glass of fresh water . . . and all I heard was her little voice, 'Don't you want any more?' That voice tinkled in my ears like a silver hurdy-gurdy! Pancracio, what about it? Shall we go back to the ranch?"

"Look here, compadre Demetrio. You may not believe it, but I've had a lot of experience with women. . . . Women! They're all right for a while. Granted! Though even that's going pretty far. You should see the scars they've given me. To hell with women. They're the devil, that's what they are! Really, compadre, don't you believe me? . . . That's why I steer clear of them. I've had a hell of a lot of experience!"

"What do you say, Pancracio? When are we going back to the ranch?" Demetrio insisted, blowing gray clouds of tobacco smoke into the air.

"Just say the word. . . . You know I left my woman there, too!"

"Your woman, hell!" Codorniz said, disgruntled and sleepy.

"Yours . . . and mine, too. It's a good thing you're kindhearted so we all can enjoy her when you bring her over," Manteca murmured.

"That's right, Pancracio, bring one-eyed María Antonia. We're all getting pretty cold around here," Meco shouted from a distance.

The crowd broke into peals of laughter, while Pancracio and Manteca vied with each other, shouting oaths and obscenities.

XX

"Villa is coming!"

The news spread like lightning.

Villa—the magic word! The Great Man, the unconquerable warrior who, even at a distance, exerts the fascination of a boa constrictor.

"Our Mexican Napoleon!" exclaims Luis Cervantes.

"Yes! The Aztec Eagle, who has buried his beak of steel in the head of Huerta the serpent!" Solís, Natera's chief of staff, remarked somewhat ironically, adding: "At least, that's how I expressed it in a speech at Ciudad Juárez!"

The two sat at the bar of the saloon, drinking beer.

The "high hats," mufflers around their necks, thick, rough leather shoes, and gnarled cowboy hands, ate and drank endlessly. All their talk was of Villa and his men.

Natera's followers won gasps of astonishment from Demetrio's men.

Villa! ... the battles of Ciudad Juárez, Tierra Blanca, Chihuahua, Torreón!

But the bare facts of the story meant nothing. You had to hear the account of his true exploits; an act of great self-sacrifice, and then one of bestial cruelty. Villa, indomitable lord of the sierra, the eternal victim of all governments; Villa tracked, hunted down like a wild beast; Villa, the reincarnation of the old legend; Villa, the generous bandit who passes through the world armed with the blazing torch of an ideal: to rob the rich and give to the poor. It was the poor who built up a legend about him which Time would embellish as a shining example from generation to generation.

"But I can tell you, my friend Montañez," one of Natera's men said, "if General Villa takes a fancy to you, he'll give you a ranch on the spot. But if he doesn't, he'll shoot you down like a dog!"

"God! You ought to see Villa's troops! They're all northerners and dressed like lords with their wide-brimmed Texas hats and their brand-new khaki suits and their four-dollar shoes, imported from the U.S.A."

As they told the wonders of Villa and his men, Natera's men gazed at one another ruefully, aware that their own hats were rotten from sunlight and moisture, that their own shirts and trousers were tattered and barely covered their grimy, lousy bodies.

"There's no such a thing as hunger up there.... They carry box-cars full of oxen, sheep, cows! They've got cars full of clothing, trains full of guns, ammunition, food enough to make a man burst!"

Then they spoke of Villa's airplanes.

"Ah, those planes! On the ground, close up, damned if you even know what they are! They look like canoes, or rafts ... but then they begin to climb, making a deafening roar. Something like an automobile racing along. Then they're like great big birds that don't even seem to move sometimes. But here's the joker! Inside that bird, an American fellow has hand grenades by the thousand. Now you go figure what that means! When it's time to fight, the American throws his lead bombs at the enemy like a farmer throws corn to his chickens. Pretty soon the whole field is nothing but a graveyard ... dead men here ... dead men there ... dead men everywhere!"

And when Anastasio Montañez asked the speaker if Natera's men had fought side by side with Villa, he realized that all this high praise was hearsay and that not a single man in Natera's army had ever laid eyes on Villa.

"Well, when you get down to it, one man's the same as the next. No man's got much more guts than any other, if you ask me. For fighting, all you need is a little pride. I'm not a professional soldier, far from it! I may be dressed like hell . . . but let me tell you . . . I don't have to be here. . . . "

"Because I own over twenty oxen, whether you believe it or not!" Codorniz said, mocking Anastasio behind his back and laughing out loud.

XXI

The gunfire lessened, then slowly died out. Luis Cervantes, who had been hiding amid a heap of ruins at the fortification on the crest of the hill, made bold to show his face.

How he had managed to hang on, he did not know. Nor did he know when Demetrio and his men had disappeared. Suddenly he had found himself alone; then, hurled back by an avalanche of infantry, he fell from his saddle; a host of men trampled over him until he stood up and a man on horseback hoisted him up behind him. But after a few moments, horse and riders fell, and without rifle, revolver, or arms of any kind, Cervantes found himself lost in the midst of white smoke and whistling bullets. A hole amid a debris of crumbling stone offered a safe haven.

"Solís!"

"Cervantes!"

"The horse threw me; they fell upon me; then they took me for dead and stole my gun. There was nothing I could do!" Luis Cervantes explained apologetically.

"Nobody threw me down," Solís said. "I'm here because I like to play safe. You know?"

The irony in Solís's voice brought a blush to Cervantes's cheek.

"By God, that chief of yours is a real man!" Solís exclaimed. "What daring, what assurance! He left me gasping—and a hell of a lot of other men with more experience than me, too!"

Luis Cervantes, confused, didn't know what to say.

"What! Weren't you there? Good for you! You found a safe place for yourself just in time. Look, pal, I'll explain; let's go behind that rock. From this slope to the foot of the hill, there's no road save this path in front of us. To the right, the incline is too sharp; you can't do anything there. And it's worse to the left; the ascent is so dangerous that a single misstep means a fall down those rocks and a broken neck at the end of it. All right! A number of us from Moya's brigade went down the slope on our bellies to attack the enemy's first line of trenches. The bullets whizzed over our heads; battle raged on all sides; for a time, they stopped firing. We thought they were being attacked from behind. We stormed their trenches. Look, partner! . . . From the middle of the slope down it's a carpet of corpses. Their machine guns did that for us. They mowed us down like wheat; only a handful escaped. The officers went white as a sheet; even though we had reinforcements, they were afraid to order a new charge. That was when Demetrio Macías, without waiting for orders from anyone, shouted, 'Come on, boys!' 'What the hell does he think he's doing!' I shouted in astonishment. The surprised officers said nothing. Macías's horse seemed to wear eagle's talons instead of hoofs, it scrambled so swiftly over the rocks. 'Come on! Come on!' his men shouted, following him over the rocks like wild deer, horses and men welded into one. Only one young fellow lost his footing and fell into the abyss. In a few seconds, the others appeared at the top of the hill, storming the trenches and stabbing the Federals. With his rope, Demetrio lassoed the machine guns and carried them off, like a bull herdsman throwing a steer. But it couldn't last. The Federals outnumbered them and could easily have destroyed Demetrio and his men. But we took advantage of their momentary confusion, rushed them and threw them out. That chief of yours is a wonderful soldier!"

Standing on the crest of the hill, they could easily see one side of La Bufa peak, with its highest crag like the feathered head of a proud Aztec king. The six-hundred-yard slope was covered with dead, their hair matted, their clothes clotted with grime and blood, and in that mountain of still-warm bodies, ragged women ranged like hungry coyotes, searching and stripping them bare.

Amid clouds of white rifle smoke and the dense, black vapors of flaming buildings, houses with wide doors and shuttered windows shone in the sunlight. The streets seemed to be piled upon one another, winding through picturesque mazes, climbing up the nearby hills. Above the graceful cluster of houses rose the lithe columns of a warehouse and the towers and cupolas of the churches.

"How beautiful the Revolution is, even in its very barbarity!" Solís said with deep feeling. Then in a low voice and with a vague melancholy:

"A pity that what remains to be done won't be as beautiful! We must wait awhile, until there are no men left to fight on either side, until no other shots are heard except for the mob ransacking and pillaging; until the psychology of our race, condensed into two words, shines like a drop of clear water: Robbery! Murder! . . . What a failure, friend, if we, who offer our enthusiasm and our lives to crush a miserable assassin, turn out to be the builders of a monstrous pedestal holding one hundred or two hundred thousand monsters of exactly the same sort. People without ideals! People born to tyranny! Vain bloodshed!"

Large groups of Federals pushed up the hill, fleeing from the "high hats."

A bullet whistled past them.

After his speech, Alberto Solís stood lost in thought, his arms crossed. Suddenly, he took fright.

"I'll be damned if I like these plaguey mosquitoes!"

Luis Cervantes smiled so scornfully that Solís calmly sat back down on a rock.

His smile wandered, following the spirals of smoke from the rifles and the dust of every demolished house and caved-in roof. He believed he discerned a symbol of the revolution in those clouds of smoke and dust that climbed upward together, embraced, became one, and disappeared into nothingness.

"Now I see what it all means!"

And his outstretched hand pointed to the train station. Locomotives belched thick columns of smoke; the trains were overloaded with fugitives who had barely managed to escape.

He felt a little blow in the stomach, and, as if his legs had turned to putty, he slid off the rock. His ears buzzed.... Then, eternal darkness and silence.

PART TWO

Demetrio, nonplussed, scratched his head: "Look here, don't ask me any more questions. I never went to school, you know. . . . You gave me the eagle I wear on my hat, didn't you? . . . All right then; you just tell me: 'Demetrio, do this or do that,' and that's all there is to it."

I

To champagne, that sparkles and foams in the flickering lamplight, Demetrio prefers Jalisco's limpid tequila.

Stained with dirt, smoke, and sweat and dressed in filthy rags, men with curly beards and disheveled hair sit in groups around the tables in a restaurant.

"I killed two colonels," one man clamors. . . . "They were so fat they couldn't even run: they tripped over the rocks and they turned as red as beets, their tongues hanging out as they climbed the hill. . . . 'Don't run so fast, *mochitos*,' I shouted at them; 'Stop, I don't care for chickens. . . . Stop, you bald-headed bums, I'm not going to hurt you. . . . Your side has surrendered!' Ha, ha, ha! . . . They fell for it! Bang, bang! One for each of them . . . and then they could finally take a rest!"

"One of their officers got away from me," says a swarthy man sitting in a corner between the wall and the bar, holding his rifle between outstretched legs. "He was wearing plenty of gold, damn him. The gold braid shone on his epaulets and his saddle blanket. And me? . . . Like an idiot I let him get away. He took out his handkerchief and gave the sign; and I stood there with my mouth wide open. I barely had time to duck and he started shooting, bullet after bullet. I let him finish off a round. . . . Then I said: 'My turn, now! Holy Virgin, Mother of God! Don't let me miss this son of a . . . But my rifle misfired . . . he was riding one fine horse, and he went by me like lightning! I took it out on the next poor bastard coming up the road. . . . I made him turn quite a somersault!"

Words fly from their mouths, and while the soldiers vie to tell their adventures, women with olive skin, bright eyes, and teeth of ivory, with revolvers at their waists, cartridge belts across their breasts, and broad hats on their heads, come and go among the groups like stray dogs.

A wench with highly rouged cheeks, dark brown arms and neck, and a coarse appearance gives a great leap and lands on the bar near Demetrio's table.

He turns his head toward her and collides with a pair of lewd eyes under a narrow forehead and thick, straight hair parted in the middle.

The door opens wide and Anastasio, Pancracio, Codorniz, and Meco file in, dazed and mouths agape.

Anastasio utters a cry of surprise and steps forward to shake hands with the fat little man wearing the *charro*[1] suit and the purple kerchief.

They are old friends, reunited, and they embrace so tightly that their faces turn color.

"Look here, compadre Demetrio, I have the pleasure of introducing you to Güero Margarito. He's a real friend. I love him like a brother. You must get to know him, chief, he's a smart man! Do you remember that jail at Escobedo, Jalisco? . . . A whole year together."

Without removing his cigar from his lips, Demetrio, buried in a sullen silence amid the bustle and the uproar, offered his hand and said:

"Pleased, I'm sure . . . "

"So your name is Demetrio Macías?" the girl asked suddenly. Seated on the bar, she swung her legs back and forth, touching Demetrio's back with the toes of her calfskin shoes.

"That's right," he answered, scarcely turning toward her.

Indifferently, she continued to swing her legs, showing off her blue stockings.

"Hey, Pintada, what are you doing here? Step down and have a drink!" said Güero Margarito.[2]

The girl accepted readily, and boldly thrust her way through a crowd and sat down facing Demetrio.

"So you're the famous Demetrio Macías, the hero of Zacatecas?" Pintada asked.

Demetrio nodded in assent, while Güero Margarito let loose a laugh and said:

"You're a smart devil, Pintada. . . . Now you want to sport a general!"

Without understanding, Demetrio raised his eyes to hers; they gazed at each other like two strange dogs sniffing one another with distrust. Demetrio could not resist her furiously provocative stare; and he lowered his eyes.

From their seats, some of Natera's officers began to hurl obscenities at Pintada.

Without paying the slightest attention, she said:

"General Natera is going to hand you out a little general's eagle. Go ahead, shake on it! . . . "

She stuck out her hand at Demetrio and shook it with the strength of a man.

Demetrio, flattered by the congratulations raining down on him, ordered champagne.

"I don't want no more to drink. I don't feel good," Güero Margarito said to the waiter. "Just bring me some ice water."

"I want something to eat," said Pancracio. "Bring me anything you've got as long as it ain't chili or beans!"

Officers kept coming in; soon the restaurant was crowded. Stars and bars showed up on hats of every kind and shape. They wore wide, silk bandannas around their necks, large diamond rings, and heavy, gold watch chains.

"Hey, waiter," Güero Margarito cried, "I ordered ice water. . . . And I'm not begging for it either, see? Look at this wad of bills; I'll buy you and . . . your old woman, understand? I don't care if it ran

out or why it ran out. . . . It's up to you to find some way to get it. I
tell you, I don't want excuses, I want my ice water. Are you bringing
it, or not? . . . No? . . . Well, take this . . ."

A heavy blow sent the waiter reeling to the floor.

"That's just the way I am, General Macías. Do you see how my
chin doesn't have a single hair on it? You know why? I'm hot tempered, and if there's no one around to pick on I tear out my own
beard until I calm down. Word of honor, General; if I didn't, I'd ex-
plode with anger."

"It's bad to let your anger eat away at you," a man affirmed
earnestly from below a hat that covered his head like a roof on a
house. "When I was up at Torreón, I killed an old lady who refused
to sell me some enchiladas. They were in demand. I got no enchiladas but I felt satisfied anyhow!"

"I killed a storekeeper at Parral because he gave me two Huerta
bills with my change," said another man with a star on his hat and
precious stones on his black, callused hands.

"Down in Chihuahua I killed a guy because I always saw him sitting at the same table at the same time when I went to eat. I just
hated the looks of him . . . what more do you want? . . ."

"Hmm! I killed . . ."

The theme is inexhaustible.

By dawn, when the restaurant is wild with joy and the floor dot-
ted with spittle, young painted girls from the suburbs mingle freely
among the dark northern women. Demetrio pulls out his jeweled
gold watch and asks Anastasio Montañez to tell him the time.

Anastasio glances at the watch, then, poking his head out of a
small window, gazes at the starry sky and says:

"The Pleiades are pretty low in the west, compadre. It won't be
long now till daybreak. . . ."

Outside the restaurant, the shouts, laughter, and songs of the
drunken men don't let up. Men gallop wildly down the streets, the
hoofs of their horses hammering on the sidewalks. From every
quarter of the town, rifle and pistol shots are heard.

Demetrio and Pintada stagger arm in arm down the center of
the street, bound for the hotel.

"What stupid fools," said Pintada, convulsed with laughter. "Where the hell are you from? Soldiers don't sleep in hotels and inns anymore. Where do you come from? You just go anywhere you like and pick a house that pleases you, and you take it without asking anyone for permission. Who's the revolution for, anyhow? For the rich folks? We're the fancy ones now.... Come on, Pancracio, hand me your bayonet. Damn these rich people!... They lock up everything they've got!"

She dug the steel point through the crack of a drawer and, pressing on the hilt, broke the lock, and opened the splinted cover of a writing desk.

Anastasio, Pancracio, and Pintada plunged their hands into a pile of letters, pictures, photographs, and papers, scattering them all over the rug.

Finding nothing he wanted, Pancracio gave vent to his anger by kicking a framed photograph into the air with the toe of his shoe. It smashed on the candelabra in the center of the room.

They pulled their empty hands out of the heap of paper, cursing.

But Pintada tirelessly continued to unlock drawer after drawer, leaving no spot unsearched.

No one noticed a small, gray, velvet-covered box that rolled silently across the floor, coming to a stop at Luis Cervantes's feet.

He, who had watched everything with profound indifference while Demetrio seemed to be asleep on the rug, pulled the box closer to himself with his foot, bent over, scratched his ankle, and deftly picked it up.

He was stunned: two flawless diamonds in a filigree setting. Hastily he hid them in his pocket.

When Demetrio awoke, Luis Cervantes said:

"General, look at the mess these boys have made here. Don't you think it would be better to avoid this sort of thing?"

"No, Curro. Poor fellows! . . . It's their only pleasure after putting their bellies up as targets for the bullets."

"Yes, of course, General, but they could do it somewhere else. You see, this sort of thing hurts our prestige, and, worse, it hurts our cause!"

Demetrio leveled his eagle eyes at Luis Cervantes. He drummed with his fingernails against his teeth and said:

"Don't blush. . . . Look, you can't fool me! . . . We know what's mine is mine and what's yours is yours. You got the box, okay; I got my gold watch."

Both of them, in perfect harmony, showed each other their booty.

Meanwhile, Pintada and her companions were ransacking the rest of the house.

Codorniz entered the room with a twelve-year-old girl whose forehead and arms were already discolored with coppery stains. They stopped short, speechless with surprise, looking at the piles of books lying on the floor, tables, and chairs; the large mirrors thrown to the ground, smashed; the huge framed prints and photographs, shattered; the furniture and bric-a-brac broken. Codorniz held his breath, his avid eyes scouring the room for booty.

Outside, in one corner of the patio, lost in dense clouds of suffocating smoke, Manteca was boiling corn on the cob, feeding his fire with books and paper that made the flames leap wildly through the air.

"Hey!" Codorniz shouted. "Look what I found! Some fine blankets for my mare!"

With a swift pull, he wrenched down a heavy drapery that fell, rod and all, on top of a handsomely carved chair.

"Look, look at all these naked women!" Codorniz's little companion cried, enchanted at a deluxe edition of Dante's *Divine Comedy.* "I like this; and I'm taking it."

She began to tear out the illustrations that pleased her most. Demetrio stood up and took a seat beside Luis Cervantes. He ordered some beer, handed one bottle to his secretary, and downed his own bottle at one gulp. Then, drowsily, he half closed his eyes, and fell back asleep.

"Hey!" a man called to Pancracio from the entry. "When can I see the General?"

"You can't see him. He's got a hangover this morning," Pancracio replied. "What do you want?"

"I want to buy some of those books you're burning."

"I'll sell them to you myself."

"How much do you want for them?"

Pancracio frowned in bewilderment.

"Give me a nickel for the ones with pictures, and the others . . . I'll give you the rest for nothing if you buy the whole lot."

The man returned with a large basket to carry away the books. . . .

"Demetrio, come on, Demetrio, wake up, already," shouted Pintada. "You're sleeping like a fat old hog! Look who's here! . . . Güero Margarito! You don't know what a fine man he is!"

"I admire you very much, General Macías, and I like the way you do things. So if it's all right, I'm going to join your brigade."

"What's your rank?" Demetrio asked him.

"I'm a captain, General."

"All right, you can serve with me now. I'll make you a major."

Güero Margarito was a round little fellow, with a waxed mustache, and cruel, blue eyes that disappeared between his fat cheeks and his forehead when he laughed. Formerly a waiter at Delmonico's in Chihuahua, now he proudly wore three small brass bars, the insignia of his rank in the Northern Division.

Güero showered Demetrio and his men with praise; and this proved sufficient reason to finish off a case of beer in short order.

Suddenly Pintada reappeared in the middle of the room, wearing a beautiful silk dress covered with exquisite lace.

"You forgot the stockings," Güero Margarito shouted, shaking with laughter.

Codorniz's girl also burst out laughing.

But Pintada didn't care; she shrugged her shoulders indifferently, sat down on the rug, kicked off her white satin slippers, and wiggled her bare toes, which had pins and needles from the tight shoes. She said:

"Hey, you, Pancracio . . . Go and get me my blue stockings . . . they're with the rest of my plunder."

The room was filling up with new friends and old comrades at arms. Demetrio, growing excited, began to narrate in detail his most notable feats of arms.

"What the hell is that noise?" he asked in surprise as he heard string and brass instruments tuning up in the patio.

"General," Luis Cervantes said solemnly, "it's a banquet all of your old friends and followers are giving in your honor to celebrate your victory at Zacatecas and your well-deserved promotion to the rank of general!"

III

"General Macías, I want you to meet my future wife," Luis Cervantes said with great emphasis as he led a beautiful girl into the dining room.

They all turned to look at her. Her large, blue eyes grew wide in wonder.

She was barely fourteen. Her skin was like a rose petal, fresh and smooth; her hair was very fair; and the expression in her eyes was partly impish curiosity, partly vague, childish fear.

Luis Cervantes noticed that Demetrio eyed her like a beast of prey, and he felt pleased with himself.

They made room for her between Luis Cervantes and Güero Margarito, opposite Demetrio.

A generous number of tequila bottles lay on the table among cut glass bowls, porcelains, and flower vases.

Meco came in, sweating and cursing, with a case of beer on his shoulder.

"You don't know that Güero yet," said Pintada, noticing that he hadn't taken his eyes off of Luis Cervantes's bride. "He's a smart fellow, I can tell you, and he never misses a trick."

She shot him a lewd look and added:

"That's why I can't stand to look at him, not even in a picture!"

The orchestra struck up a raucous march as though they were playing at a bullfight.

The soldiers roared with joy.

"What fine tripe, General! . . . I swear I haven't tasted the like of it in all my life," Güero Margarito said, as he began to reminisce about Delmonico's in Chihuahua.

"You really like it, Güero?" responded Demetrio. "Go ahead, call for more, eat your bellyful."

"It's just the way I like it," Anastasio Montañez chimed in, "and that's the best part—when food tastes so good it . . . it makes me belch."

The noise of mouths being filled and ravenous feeding followed. All drank copiously.

At the end of the dinner, Luis Cervantes picked up a champagne glass and rose to his feet:

"General . . . "

"Whoa!" Pintada interrupted. "Speech making isn't for me. I might as well head for the corral since there's nothing more to eat here."

Luis Cervantes presented the small brass eagle on its black-cloth escutcheon with a toast that no one understood but everyone applauded enthusiastically.

Demetrio took the insignia of his new rank in his hands and, face flushed and eyes shining, declared with great candor:

"What am I going to do now with this buzzard!"

"Compadre," Anastasio Montañez said in a tremulous voice. "I don't have to tell you . . . "

Whole minutes elapsed; the cursed words would not come to Anastasio. His face turned crimson, the perspiration beading up on his dirt-encrusted forehead. Finally he decided to finish his toast at all costs.

"Well, I don't have to tell you . . . you've always known I'm your compadre. . . . "

And, since everyone had applauded for Luis Cervantes, Anasta-

sio himself, having finished, gave the signal by clapping his hands
solemnly.

But everything turned out for the best, since his awkwardness
inspired others. Manteca and Codorniz stood up and made their
toasts, too.

When Meco's turn came, Pintada rushed in, shouting jubilantly.
Clicking her tongue, she tried to drag a splendid black horse into
the dining room.

"My booty! My booty!" she cried, patting the superb animal on
the neck.

The mare resisted coming through the door; but a strong jerk of
the rope and a sudden lash brought her in, prancing smartly.

The soldiers, half drunk, stared at the fine catch with ill-
disguised envy.

"I don't know what the hell this she-devil's got, but she always
beats everybody to it," cried Güero Margarito. "She's been the
same ever since she joined us at Tierra Blanca!"

"Hey, Pancracio, go and get me some alfalfa for my mare," Pintada commanded crisply.

Then she threw the horse's rope to one of the soldiers.

Once more they filled their glasses. Some were beginning to nod
their heads and close their eyes; but most of the company shouted
with glee.

Luis Cervantes's girl, who had spilled all her wine on a handkerchief, looked about her with wide, blue, wondering eyes.

"Boys," Güero suddenly screamed, his shrill, guttural voice
dominating the uproar, "I'm tired of living; I feel like killing myself
right now. I'm sick and tired of Pintada ... and this other little angel
from heaven won't even look at me!"

Luis Cervantes saw that the last remark was addressed to his
girlfriend; with great surprise he realized that it was not Demetrio's
foot he had felt close to the girl's, but Güero Margarito's.

He was boiling with indignation.

"Keep your eye on me, boys," Güero went on, gun in hand. "I'm
going to shoot myself right in the forehead!"

He aimed at the large mirror on the opposite wall, which gave back his whole body in reflection.

"Don't move, Pintada!"

The mirror broke into large jagged fragments. The bullet had grazed Pintada's hair, but she didn't even blink.

IV

Late in the afternoon, Luis Cervantes rubbed his eyes and sat up. He found himself on the hard ground in the garden among the flowerpots. Anastasio, Pancracio, and Codorniz were sleeping nearby, breathing heavily.

His lips were swollen, his nose dry and cold; he saw bloodstains on his hands and shirt, and at once he recalled what had happened. Quickly he rose to his feet and made for one of the bedrooms. He pushed at the door several times without being able to force it open. For a few minutes he stood there, hesitating.

Because it was all true; he was sure he hadn't been dreaming. He had left the table with his young companion; he took her to the bedroom; but just as he was closing the door, Demetrio, staggering drunkenly, rushed after them. Then Pintada followed Demetrio and began to struggle with him. Demetrio, his eyes white-hot, his lips wet with spittle, looked eagerly for the young girl. Pintada pushed him back vigorously.

"What the hell . . . ? What do you think you're doing?" he howled in annoyance.

Pintada put her leg between his, twisted it suddenly, and Demetrio fell flat on the ground outside of the bedroom. He got up, enraged.

"Help! Help! He's going to kill me!"

Pintada seized Demetrio's wrist, and turned the gun aside.

The bullet dug into the bricks. Pintada continued bellowing. Anastasio Montañez disarmed Demetrio from behind.

Demetrio, standing like a furious bull in the middle of the arena, cast fierce glances at all sides. Cervantes, Anastasio, Manteca, and the others surrounded him.

"Bastards! You've taken my gun away! As if I needed a gun to beat the hell out of you."

Flinging out his arms, in a few seconds he felled everyone within reach. And after that? Luis Cervantes could remember nothing more. Surely they had stayed there all night beaten and asleep. Surely his girlfriend, terrified by all those brutes, had wisely hidden herself away.

"Perhaps this bedroom connects to the living room and I can go in through there," he thought.

At the sound of his footsteps, Pintada woke up. She was sleeping on the rug close to Demetrio, at the foot of a couch filled with alfalfa and corn where the black mare was feeding.

"What are you looking for?" the girl asked. "Oh, I know what you want! Shame on *you*! Why, I had to lock up your sweetheart because I couldn't hold back this damned Demetrio anymore. Grab the key, it's lying on that table, there!"

Luis Cervantes searched every nook and cranny in vain.

"Come on, Curro, don't worry. I'll give it to you. But tell me; I like to hear about these things. That girl is just your type. She's not a country hick like us."

"I've nothing to tell. She's my fiancée and that's all."

"Ho! Ho! Ho! Your fiancée, huh? Look, Curro, I've been around the block a few times myself. I'm an old hand at this. It was Meco and Manteca who took that poor girl from her home; I knew that all along . . . but you must have given them something for her, a pair of cuff links or a miraculous picture of the Virgin of Guadalupe. . . .

Am I right? ... There are a few smart folks around here. The trick is finding them. ... Right?"

Pintada got up to give him the key, but to her surprise she couldn't find it either.

She stood there a long while, thinking. All of a sudden she ran to the bedroom door and peered through the keyhole, standing motionless until her eye got used to the dark. Then, without drawing away, she murmured:

"Oh, Güero! Son of a ...! Come here and take a look, Curro!"

And she walked away, laughing loudly.

"Didn't I tell you I'd never seen a smarter fellow in all my life!"

The following morning, Pintada watched for the moment when Güero left the bedroom to feed his horses:

"Come on, Angel Face. Run home quick! These fellows might kill you. ... Go ahead, run! ... "

Pintada threw Manteca's flea-ridden blanket over the girl with the big, blue eyes and a face like a Madonna, and who was wearing only her chemise and stockings. She grabbed her by the hand and put her out on the street.

"Thank God!" she cried. "Everything's okay now. I'm crazy about that Güero!"

V

Like colts neighing and frisking in the first rains of May, Demetrio's men gallop through the sierra.

"To Moyahua, boys. To Demetrio Macías's country!"

"To the land of Don Mónico, the *cacique*."

The landscape grows brighter; the sun appears in a scarlet band across the diaphanous sky.

Like the bony spines of immense sleeping monsters, the chains of mountains rise in the distance. Hills like the heads of colossal Aztec idols; like giants' faces, their grimaces awe-inspiring and grotesque, calling for a smile or a shudder at a presentiment of mystery.

Demetrio Macías rides at the head of his men with the members of his staff: Colonel Anastasio Montañez, Lieutenant Colonel Pancracio, Majors Luis Cervantes and Güero Margarito.

Next in line come Pintada and Venancio, who pays her many compliments and recites the despairing verses of Antonio Plaza.[1]

As the sun's rays began to tint the stone walls of the houses, they made their entrance into Moyahua, four abreast, to the sound of the bugle.

The roosters' chorus was deafening, dogs barked their alarm; but not a living soul stirred on the streets.

Pintada spurred her black mare and with one jump was abreast with Demetrio. Proudly she wore a silk dress and heavy gold earrings; her pale blue gown emphasized the olive tone of her face and the coppery stains on her weathered skin. Riding astride, she had pulled her skirts up to her knees; and her stockings showed, filthy and full of runs. She wore a gun at her breast, and a cartridge belt hung over the pommel of her saddle.

Demetrio was also dressed in his best clothes. His broadbrimmed hat was richly embroidered; his chamois trousers were adorned with silver buttons; his coat, embroidered with gold thread.

There was a sound of doors being forced open.

The soldiers had already scattered through the town and were gathering up ammunition and saddles from everywhere.

"We're going to bid Don Mónico good morning," Demetrio said gravely, dismounting and tossing his reins to one of his men. "We're going to have breakfast with Don Mónico, who's a particular friend of mine. . . . "

The general's staff smiled with a sinister smirk.

Dragging their spurs along the sidewalks, they headed toward a large, pretentious house that could only belong to a *cacique*.

"It's closed up tight," Anastasio Montañez said, pushing the door with all his might.

"I know how to open it," Pancracio answered, immediately aiming his rifle at the lock.

"No, no," Demetrio said, "knock first."

Three blows with the butt of the rifle; three more, and no answer. Pancracio grows haughty and doesn't pay attention to orders. He fires, smashing the lock, and the door opens.

They see the hems of skirts and children's legs hurrying farther into the house.

"I want wine! . . . Serve up some wine!" Demetrio demands in an imperious voice, pounding heavily on a table.

"Sit down, boys."

A lady peeps out, then another, and a third; and among the black skirts, the heads of frightened children appear. One of the women, trembling, walks toward a cupboard, takes out some glasses and a bottle, and serves the wine.

"What weapons do you have?" Demetrio demands harshly.

"Weapons?..." the lady answers, tongue-tied. "What weapons do you expect a few respectable ladies to have, who are here all by ourselves?"

"All alone, eh! Where's Señor Mónico?"

"He's not here, gentlemen. We merely rent the house from him.... We only know him by name!"

Demetrio orders his men to search the house.

"No, please. We'll bring you whatever we have ourselves, but please for God's sake, don't harm us. We're decent women, spinsters."

"What about these kids here?" Pancracio interrupts brutally. "Did they spring from the earth?"

The women disappear hurriedly and return a moment later with an old shotgun, covered with dust and cobwebs, and a pistol with rusty, broken springs.

Demetrio smiles.

"All right, then, let's see the money...."

"Money? But what money do you think a few lonely spinsters have?"

They glance up in supplication at the nearest soldier; but then they close their eyes in horror. For they have just seen the Roman soldier who crucified Our Lord in the *Vía Crucis* of the parish! They have seen Pancracio!...

Demetrio orders the search.

Once again the women disappear and return this time with a moth-eaten wallet containing a few Huerta bills.

Demetrio smiles and, without further delay, has his men come in.

Like hungry dogs who have sniffed their prey, the mob bursts in, trampling down the women who seek to bar the entrance with their bodies. Several fall into a faint; others flee in panic; the children scream.

Pancracio is about to break the lock of a huge wardrobe when the doors open and out jumps a man with a rifle in his hands.

"Don Mónico!" they all exclaim in surprise.

"Demetrio!... Don't do anything to me!... Please don't hurt me! Don Demetrio! I'm your friend!"

Demetrio Macías laughs slyly and asks if he always receives his friends at gunpoint.

Don Mónico, in consternation, throws himself at Demetrio's feet, clasps his knees, kisses his shoes:

"My wife!... My children!... Please, Don Demetrio, my friend!"

Demetrio, his hand quivering, puts his gun back in the holster.

A painful silhouette has crossed his mind. A woman with a child in her arms, walking over the rocks of the sierra in the moonlight.... A house in flames....

"Let's go!... Everybody outside!" he orders darkly.

His staff obeys. Don Mónico and the ladies kiss his hands and weep with gratitude.

The mob in the street, talking and laughing, waits for the general's permission to ransack the *cacique*'s house.

"I know where they've buried their money but I won't tell," says a youngster with a basket under his arm.

"Hm! I know, too," says an old woman carrying a burlap sack to hold "whatever the good Lord will provide." "It's on top of something ... there's a lot of trinkets and among the trinkets there's a small bag with mother-of-pearl around it. That's the thing to look for!"

"That can't be," puts in a man. "They ain't such fools to leave silver lying loose like that. I'm thinking they've got it buried in the well, in a leather bag."

The mob moves slowly; some carry ropes to tie about their bundles, others wooden trays; the women open out their aprons or shawls calculating how much can fit. All give thanks to Divine Providence as they wait for their share of the booty.

When Demetrio announces that he will not allow looting, and orders them to disband, the mob, disconsolate, obeys him, and soon scatters; but there is a dull murmur of discontent among the soldiers and no one moves from his place.

Annoyed, Demetrio repeats this order.

A young man, a recent recruit, his head turned by drink, laughs and walks boldly toward the door.

But before he can cross the threshold, a shot lays him low like a bull pierced by the matador's sword.

Motionless, his smoking gun in his hand, Demetrio waits for the soldiers to withdraw.

"Set fire to the house!" he ordered Luis Cervantes when they reached their quarters.

With a curious eagerness, Luis Cervantes did not transmit the order but undertook the task in person.

Two hours later, when the town square was black with smoke and enormous tongues of fire rose from Don Mónico's house, no one could account for the strange behavior of the general.

VI

They had taken quarters in a large, gloomy house belonging to the same *cacique* of Moyahua.

The previous occupants had already left their mark in the patio, converted into a manure pile; on the chipped walls, which revealed the bare adobe; on the floors, torn up by the hoofs of animals; in the orchard, littered with withered leaves and dry branches. Upon entering, one stumbled over the legs of furniture, seats and backs of chairs, all covered with dirt and refuse.

By ten o'clock, Luis Cervantes yawned with boredom, and said good night to Güero Margarito and Pintada, who were downing endless drinks on a bench in the square.

He made for the barracks. The drawing room was the only room still furnished. He entered, and Demetrio, who was lying on the floor with his eyes wide open staring at the ceiling, stopped trying to count the beams and turned to look at him.

"That you, Curro? . . . What's new? Come on in, sit down."

Luis Cervantes first went over to trim the candle, then he drew up a chair without a back, a coarse rag doing the duty of a wicker bottom. The legs of the chair squeaked; and Pintada's black mare snorted, moving in the shadows and tracing a graceful curve with her sleek, round haunches.

Luis Cervantes sank into his seat and said:

"General, I wish to make my report. Here you have ... "

"Look here, man ... I didn't really want this. ... Moyahua is almost my hometown. They'll say this is why we've been fighting!" Demetrio replied, looking at the bulging sack of coins that Luis was handing to him.

Cervantes left his seat to squat down by Demetrio's side. He spread a blanket out on the floor and onto it poured a bag of ten-peso pieces, shining like golden embers.

"First of all, General, only you and I know about this. ... Second, you know well enough that if the sun shines, you should open the window. It's shining on us now, but what about tomorrow? You should always look ahead. A bullet, a bolting horse, even a ridiculous head cold . . . , and then there are a widow and orphans left in absolute want! . . . The Government? Ha! Ha! . . . Just go see Carranza or Villa or any of the big chiefs and try and tell them about your family. . . . If they answer with a kick in the you know what, say it's fine with you. And they're right; we didn't rise up in arms to make some Carranza or Villa President of our Republic. No, we're fighting to defend the sacred rights of the people that are trampled on by the miserable *cacique*. And so, just as Villa and Carranza aren't going to ask our consent for the payment they're getting for the services they're rendering the country, we don't have to ask anybody's permission either."

Demetrio half stood up, grasped a bottle that stood nearby, drained it, and then puffed out his cheeks and spat the liquor across the room.

"Curro, you've certainly got the gift of gab!"

Luis felt dizzy. The spattered beer seemed to intensify the stench of refuse on which they were sitting: a carpet of orange and banana peels, fleshy watermelon rind, stringy masses of mangoes and sugarcane, all mixed up with cornhusks from tamales and damp with human waste.

Demetrio's callused fingers shuffled through the brilliant coins, counting and counting.

Recovering from his nausea, Luis Cervantes pulled out a small box of Fallières phosphate and poured out lockets, rings, earrings, and countless valuable jewels.

"Look here, General, if as it seems, this mess continues, if the revolution doesn't end, we already have enough to leave the country for a while and live quite comfortably." Demetrio shook his head. "You wouldn't do that? . . . Well, what would we stick around for then? . . . What cause would we be defending?"

"That's something I can't explain, Curro; but I'm thinking it wouldn't show much guts. . . . "

"Take your choice, General," said Luis Cervantes, pointing to the jewels, which he had set in a row.

"Oh, you keep it all. . . . Really, Curro. If you could only see that I don't care for money. Want me to tell you the truth? I'm the happiest man in the world, so long as I've got something to drink and a nice little wench that catches my eye. . . . "

"Ha! Ha! You're a card, General. Why do you stand for that snake Pintada, then?"

"I'll tell you, Curro, I'm fed up with her, but I'm like that. I can't get up the nerve to tell her so. I don't have the courage to send her to . . . That's the way I am. When I like a woman, I get tongue-tied, and if she doesn't start something, I don't dare to either." He sighed. "There's Camilla at the ranch for instance. . . . The girl's ugly; but if you could only see how she pleases me."

"Well, General, we'll go and get her any day you like."

Demetrio winked maliciously.

"I promise you I'll do it, General."

"Do you really mean it, Curro? Look here, if you pull that off for me, I'll give you the gold watch and chain you're hankering after."

Luis Cervantes's eyes shone. He took the phosphate box, heavy with its contents, and stood up smiling.

"I'll see you tomorrow," he said. "Good night, General! Sleep well."

VII

"What do I know? Just the same as you all. The General told me, 'Codorniz, saddle your horse and my dappled mare. You're going on an errand with Curro.' Well, that's what happened. We left here at noon, and reached the ranch at nightfall. One-eyed María Antonia took us in. . . . She asked after you, Pancracio. Next morning, Luis Cervantes woke me up. 'Codorniz, Codorniz, saddle the horses. Leave me mine but take the General's mare back to Moyahua. I'll catch up after a bit.' The sun was high when he reached me with Camilla riding behind him. She got off and we mounted her on the dappled mare."

"Well, and her? What sort of a face was she wearing?" one of the men inquired.

"Hm! She was so damned happy she was gabbing all the way."

"And Curro?"

"Just as quiet as ever, the way he always is."

"I think," Venancio expressed his opinion with great seriousness, "that if Camilla woke up in the General's bed, it was just a mistake. We drank a lot, remember! . . . That alcohol went to our heads; we must have lost our senses."

"What the hell do you mean, alcohol! . . . It was all cooked up between Cervantes and the General."

"Certainly! That city dude's nothing but a . . ."

"I don't like to talk about friends behind their backs," said Güero Margarito, "but I can tell you this: of the two sweethearts he's had, one was mine, and the other was for the General."

They burst into guffaws of laughter.

When Pintada realized what had happened, she went to Camilla and comforted her affectionately.

"Poor little child! Tell me how all this happened."

Camilla's eyes were swollen from weeping.

"He lied to me! He lied! . . . He came to the ranch and he told me, 'Camilla, I came just to get you. Do you want to go away with me?' You bet I wanted to go with him. As far as loving him goes, I love him something fierce. . . . Look how thin I've grown just pining away for him. In the morning I don't feel like grinding corn. . . . Mama calls me to lunch and the tortilla has no taste . . ."

Once more she burst into tears, stuffing the corner of her shawl into her mouth to drown her sobs.

"Look here, I'll help you out of this mess. Don't be silly, child, don't cry. Don't think about that Curro anymore! You know what he is. . . . I swear! . . . That's the only reason why the General stands for him. What a goose! . . . All right, you want to go back home?"

"The Holy Virgin of Jalpa protect me. . . . My mother would beat me to death!"

"She'll do nothing of the sort. You and I can fix things. The soldiers are leaving any moment now. When Demetrio tells you to get ready, you tell him you feel pains all over your body as though someone had hit you; and you lie right down and yawn. Then put your hand on your forehead and say, 'I'm burning up with fever.' I'll tell Demetrio to leave us both here, that I'll stay to take care of you, that as soon as you're feeling all right again, we'll catch up with them. But instead of that, I'll see that you get home safe and sound."

VIII

The sun had already set, and the town was wrapped in the drab melancholy of its ancient streets amid the frightened silence of its inhabitants, who had retired very early, when Luis Cervantes reached Primitivo's general store, interrupting a party that promised great doings. Demetrio was getting drunk with his old comrades. Not another person could fit at the bar. Demetrio, Pintada, and Güero Margarito had tied up their horses outside; but the other officers had stormed in brutally, horses and all. Embroidered hats with enormous, concave brims bobbed up and down everywhere. The horses wheeled about, tossing their fine heads with their large, black eyes, flaring nostrils, and small ears. Over the infernal din of the drunkards was heard the heavy breathing of the horses, the stamp of their hoofs on the tiled floor, and, occasionally, a quick, nervous whinny.

A trivial episode was being commented upon when Luis Cervantes came in. A civilian with a round, black, bloody hole in his forehead lay stretched out, face up, in the middle of the street. Opinion was at first divided, but finally all concurred with Güero Margarito's sound reasoning. The poor devil lying out there dead was the church sexton. . . . But what an idiot! . . . His own fault, of course! . . . Who in the name of hell could be so foolish as to dress up in trousers, coat, cap, and all? Pancracio simply could not bear the sight of a dandy in front of him!

Eight musicians, their faces as red and round as suns, their eyes popping from blowing their lungs out since dawn, interrupt their labors at Cervantes's command.

"General," he said pushing his way through the men on horseback, "a messenger has just arrived with urgent news. You are ordered to leave immediately in pursuit of Orozco[1] and his men."

Faces that had been dark and gloomy lit up with joy.

"To Jalisco, boys!" cried Güero Margarito, pounding on the counter.

"Make ready, all you darling Jalisco girls, for I'm coming, too!" Codorniz shouted, twisting back the brim of his hat.

The enthusiasm and rejoicing were general. Demetrio's friends, in the excitement of drunkenness, offered to join his troops. Demetrio was so happy that he could scarcely speak. They were going to fight Orozco and his men! . . . At last, they would pit themselves against real men! No more shooting down Federals like so many rabbits or wild turkeys.

"If I could get hold of Pascual Orozco alive," Güero Margarito said, "I'd rip off the soles of his feet and make him walk twenty-four hours over the sierra!"

"Was that the guy who killed Madero?" asked Meco.

"No," Güero Margarito replied solemnly, "but once when I was a waiter at Delmonico's up in Chihuahua, he hit me in the face!"

"Give Camilla the dappled mare," Demetrio ordered Pancracio, who was already saddling the horses.

"Camilla can't go!" said Pintada promptly.

"Who asked for your opinion?" Demetrio retorted angrily.

"It's true, isn't it, Camilla? You woke up sore all over, and you've got a fever right now?"

"Well . . . anything Demetrio says."

"Don't be a fool! Say 'No,' come on, say 'No,'" Pintada whispered nervously into Camilla's ear.

"Well, it's just that I'm starting to like him. . . . Would you believe it!" Camilla whispered back.

Pintada turned purple, her cheeks swelled; but, without a word, she went off to get her horse that Güero Margarito was saddling.

IX

The whirlwind of dust, which stretched a long way down the road, suddenly broke into violent, diffuse masses; and there emerged broad chests, tangled manes, quivering nostrils, spirited oval eyes, hoofs flying in the air, legs stiffened from endless galloping. Men with bronze faces, ivory teeth, and flashing eyes brandished their rifles or slung them across the saddles.

Demetrio and Camilla brought up the rear. She was still nervous, white-lipped, and parched; he was angry at their futile maneuver. Neither Orozco's men nor any kind of battle. A handful of routed Federals, and a poor devil of a priest and a hundred misguided followers beneath the banner "Religion and Church's Rights."[1] The priest remained behind, dangling from a mesquite tree, and, on the field, a stream of dead men who were wearing red, cloth insignias with the motto, "Halt! The Sacred Heart of Jesus is with me!"

"One good thing about it is that I've collected all my back pay, and then some," Codorniz said, exhibiting the gold watches and rings stolen from the priest's house.

"It's fun fighting this way," Manteca cried, spicing every other word with an oath. "You know why the hell you're risking your hide!"

In the same hand with which he held the reins, he clutched a shining ornament that he had torn from the Divine Prisoner in the church.

When Codorniz, an expert in such matters, examined Manteca's treasure covetously, he uttered a solemn guffaw.

"Your ornament is nothing but tin!"

"Why are you lugging around that scum?" Pancracio asked Güero Margarito, who appeared dragging a prisoner.

"Know why? Because I've never had a good look at a man's face when a rope tightens around his neck!"

The fat prisoner breathed with difficulty; his face was sunburnt, his eyes red, and his forehead dripped with sweat. He was on foot, with his wrists bound together.

"Here, Anastasio, lend me your lasso. Mine's not strong enough; this bird will ... No, I've changed my mind. ... I think I'll kill you once and for all; you're suffering too much. Look, all the mesquites are still a long way off and there's not even a telegraph pole to hang you."

Güero Margarito pulled his gun out, pressed the muzzle against the prisoner's left breast, and brought his finger against the trigger slowly ... slowly. ...

The Federal turned pale as a corpse; his face lengthened; his eyes were fixed in a glassy stare. His chest heaved and his whole body shook as if with a chill.

Güero Margarito kept his gun in the same position for a moment as long as all eternity. His eyes shone queerly, and an expression of supreme pleasure lit up his fat, puffy face.

"No, my Federal friend," he drawled, putting his gun back into the holster, "I'm not going to kill you just yet. ... I'll make you my orderly. You'll see that I'm not so hard-hearted!"

Slyly he winked at his companions.

The prisoner was stupefied; all he could do was make gulping sounds; his mouth and throat were dry.

Camilla, who had stayed behind, spurred her mare and caught up with Demetrio.

"What a brute that Margarito is; you ought to see what he's doing to a wretched prisoner."

Then she told Demetrio what she had just seen.

The latter wrinkled his brow but made no answer.

Pintada called Camilla aside.

"Hey you ... what are you gabbing about? Güero Margarito's my sweetheart, understand? Now you know. . . . His business is my business. I'm warning you!"

Camilla, frightened, hurried to catch up with Demetrio.

X

The troops camped in a field, near three small, lone houses standing in a row, their white walls cutting the purple sash of the horizon.

Demetrio and Camilla rode toward them.

Inside the corral a man, clad in a white shirt and trousers, stood greedily puffing at a cornhusk cigarette. Nearby, another man sat on a flat stone shelling corn, rubbing the cobs between his hands; and, kicking the air with one dry, withered leg that ended in something like a goat's hoof, he frightened the chickens away.

"Hurry up, 'Pifanio," said the one who was standing up, "the sun has gone down already and you still haven't taken the animals to water."

A horse neighed outside the corral, and both men lifted their heads in amazement.

Demetrio and Camilla were peering over the corral wall at them.

"I just want a place to sleep for my woman and me," Demetrio said reassuringly.

And because he explained that he was the chief of a small army that was to camp nearby that night, the man smoking, who owned the place, bid them enter, with great deference. He ran to fetch a

broom and a pail of water to sweep and wash the best corner of the
hut as decent lodging for his distinguished guests.

"Hurry up, 'Pifanio, go out there and unsaddle the horses."

The man who was shelling corn stood up with an effort. He was
clad in a tattered shirt and vest, and torn trousers, split at the seam,
like two wings dangling from his waist.

As he walked, his gait marked a grotesque rhythm.

"But, friend, are you able to work?" Demetrio asked, refusing to
allow him to touch the saddles.

"Poor man," the owner shouted from within the hut, "he's lost all
his strength.... But you should see how he works for his pay.... He
starts working the minute God above rises in the morning! . . . It's
after sundown now . . . and look at him, hasn't stopped yet!"

Demetrio went out with Camilla for a stroll about the encampment. The field, golden, furrowed, stripped even of the smallest
bushes, extended limitless in its desolation. The three tall ash trees
that stood in front of the small houses, with their dark green crests,
round and waving, their rich foliage, drooping to kiss the ground,
seemed a veritable miracle.

"I don't know why, but I feel there's a lot of sadness here," said
Demetrio.

"Yes," Camilla answered, "I feel that way, too."

On the bank of a small stream, 'Pifanio was strenuously tugging
at the rope of a windlass. He poured a huge jar of water over a heap
of freshly cut grass, and, in the twilight, the stream of water shim-
mered as it overflowed the trough. A thin cow, a scrawny nag, and a
burro drank noisily together.

Demetrio recognized the lame peon and asked him:

"How much do you get a day, friend?"

"Eight cents, boss."

He was a little, scrofulous, fair man with blue eyes and straight hair.

He complained bitterly about the boss, the ranch, and his bad
luck.

"You certainly earn your pay all right, my lad," Demetrio interrupted kindly. "You complain and complain, but you work and
work."

Turning to Camilla:

"There're always others worse off than us mountainfolk, right?"

"Yes!" Camilla replied.

They went on.

The valley was lost in shadow, and the stars were hidden.

Demetrio put his arm around Camilla's waist amorously and whispered in her ear.

"Yes," she answered in a faint voice.

She was indeed beginning to fall for him.

—

Demetrio slept badly and shot out of the house very early.

"Something is going to happen to me," he thought.

It was a silent dawn, with faint murmurs of joy. A thrush chirped timidly in an ash tree; the animals in the corral rummaged through the refuse; the pig grunted sleepily. The orange tints of the sun appeared, and the last star flickered out.

Demetrio walked slowly to the encampment.

He was thinking of his yoke of oxen—two young, black beasts with just two years working the fields—of his two acres of well-fertilized corn. The face of his young wife came to his mind, clear and true as life: sweet features, infinitely gentle for her husband, forceful and proud toward strangers. But when he tried to conjure up the image of his son, his efforts were in vain; he had forgotten him.

He reached the camp. Stretched out among the furrows, the soldiers slept with the horses, heads bowed, eyes close.

"Our horses are pretty tired, compadre Anastasio. I think we ought to stay here at least another day."

"Oh, compadre Demetrio! . . . I'm hankering for the sierra. . . . If you only knew. . . . You may not believe me, but nothing strikes me right here. I feel sad . . . blue . . . who knows what it is that's missing here."

"How many hours' ride from here to Limón?"

"It's not a matter of hours; it's three days' hard riding, compadre Demetrio."

Pintada didn't wait long to go and look for Camilla.

"Hey, what do you know! . . . Demetrio's going to leave you flat! He told me so himself. He's going to bring his real wife. And she's very pretty, very fair . . . such rosy cheeks. . . . But if you still don't want to leave, I suppose they could use you: they've got a child, and you could carry it around. . . ."

When Demetrio returned, Camilla, weeping, told him everything.

"Don't pay no attention to that crazy woman. It's all lies, lies. . . ."

And since Demetrio did not go to Limón or remember his wife again, Camilla was quite content, and Pintada turned angry as a scorpion.

XI

Before dawn, they left for Tepatitlán. Scattered along the main road and the fields, their silhouettes wavered indistinctly to the monotonous, rhythmic gait of their horses, then faded away in the pearly light of the waning moon that bathed the whole valley.

Dogs barked in the distance.

"By noon we'll reach Tepatitlán, Cuquío tomorrow, and then . . . on to the sierra!" Demetrio said.

"Don't you think it advisable to go to Aguascalientes[1] first, General?" Luis Cervantes whispered.

"What for?"

"We're running low on funds."

"What! . . . Forty thousand pesos in eight days!"

"Just this week we recruited almost five hundred new men; all the money's gone in advance loans and gratuities," Luis Cervantes answered in a low voice.

"No! We'll go straight to the sierra. We'll see later on."

"Yes, to the sierra!" many of the men shouted.

"To the sierra! To the sierra! Hurrah for the mountains!"

The plains were oppressive to them; they spoke with enthusiasm, almost with delirium, of the sierra; and they thought about her the way they would a beloved mistress whom they hadn't seen for a long time.

Dawn broke, then a cloud of fine, reddish dust rose toward the east in an immense curtain of fiery purple.

Luis Cervantes pulled in his reins and waited for Codorniz.

"What's the last word on our deal, Codorniz?"

"I told you, Curro, two hundred for the watch alone."

"No! I'll buy the whole lot: watches, rings, and all the jewels. How much?"

Codorniz hesitated, turned pale; then he said impetuously:

"Two thousand in bills, for the whole business!"

But Luis Cervantes gave himself away. His eyes shone with such an obvious greed that Codorniz recanted and exclaimed:

"No. I was just fooling you. I won't sell nothing! Just the watch, see? And that's only because I owe Pancracio two hundred. He beat me at cards last night!"

Luis Cervantes pulled out four crisp bills of Villa's issue and placed them in Codorniz's hands.

"I'd like to buy the lot. . . . Besides, nobody will offer you more than that!"

As the sun began to beat down upon them, Manteca suddenly shouted:

"Güero Margarito, your orderly says he wants to cash in his chips. He says he can't walk anymore."

The prisoner had fallen in the middle of the road, utterly exhausted.

"Well, well!" Güero Margarito shouted, retracing his steps. "So, you're all tired out, my charming fellow. Poor little you! I'll buy a glass case and keep you in a corner of my house just like Baby Jesus. But first you've got to make it to town, and for that I'm going to help you."

He drew his sword and struck the unfortunate man several times.

"Let's have a look at your lariat, Pancracio," he said, with a strange gleam in his eyes. But when Codorniz observed that the prisoner no longer moved arm or leg, he burst into a loud guffaw:

"What a fool I am! . . . Just when I had him trained to do without food, too!"

———

"This is it, we're almost to Guadalajara," Venancio said, noticing the smiling row of houses in Tepatitlán nestled against the hillside.

They entered joyously. Rosy cheeks and beautiful, dark eyes appeared at the windows.

The schools were quickly converted into barracks. Demetrio found lodging in the sacristy of an abandoned church.

Then the soldiers scattered about, as usual, looking for loot under the pretext of gathering up arms and horses.

In the afternoon, some of Demetrio's men lay stretched out in the courtyard of the church, scratching their bellies. Venancio, his chest and shoulders bare, was gravely occupied in picking fleas from his shirt.

A man drew near the wall, asking permission to speak to the commander.

The soldiers raised their heads, but no one answered.

"I'm a widower, gentlemen. I've got nine children and I barely make a living with the sweat of my brow. . . . Don't be so hard on us poor folk."

"Don't you worry about women, Uncle," said Meco, who was rubbing his feet with tallow, "we've got Pintada here with us; you can have her for cost."

The man smiled bitterly.

"She's only got one fault," Pancracio observed, lying face up, staring at the blue sky, "she hardly looks at a man and she's already in heat."

They laughed loudly; but Venancio, with utmost gravity, pointed to the sacristy door.

The stranger entered timidly and confided his troubles to Demetrio. The soldiers had cleaned him out; they had not left a single grain of corn.

"Why did you let them?" Demetrio asked indolently.

The man persisted, lamenting and weeping, and Luis Cervantes was about to throw him out with an insult. But Camilla intervened.

"Come on, Don Demetrio, don't be harsh, give an order for him to get his corn back! . . ."

Luis Cervantes was obliged to obey; he wrote a few lines, and Demetrio put his illegible scrawl at the bottom.

"May God repay you, my child! God will lead you to heaven that you may enjoy his glory. Sixteen bushels of corn are barely enough for this year's food!" the man cried, weeping for gratitude. Then he took the paper and kissed everybody's hand.

XII

They had almost reached Cuquío, when Anastasio Montañez rode up to Demetrio and said:

"Listen, compadre, I almost forgot to tell you. . . . What a joker that Güero is! You know what he did with that old man who came to complain about the corn we'd taken for our horses? Well, he went to the barracks with the paper you gave him. 'Right you are, brother, come in,' Güero said. 'Come on in, it's only right to give you back what's yours. How many bushels did we steal? Fifteen? Sure it wasn't more than fifteen? . . . That's right, about twenty, eh? Or was it forty, perhaps? . . . Try and remember. . . . You're a poor man, and you've lots of kids to raise. . . . Yes, it must have been the thirty bushels right over there. . . . Come along; it's not just ten or fifteen or twenty I'm going to give you. You're going to count them for yourself. . . . One, two, three . . . and when you've had enough you just tell me and I'll stop.' And he pulled out his sword and beat him until he cried for mercy."

Pintada doubled over in laughter.

And Camilla, unable to control herself, blurted out:

"Hateful old man! I can't stand the sight of him!"

At once Pintada's expression changed.

"What the hell is it to you!"

Camilla, frightened, spurred her mare forward.

Pintada urged hers ahead, too, and, pushing roughly past Camilla, she grabbed her by the head and undid her long braid.

The shoving made Camilla's mare rear up, and the girl let go of the reins to push her hair out of her face; she hesitated, lost her balance, and fell against the stones, cutting open her forehead.

Pintada, overcome with laughter, galloped on with utmost skill and caught the loose mare.

"Come on, Curro; here's a job for you," Pancracio said when he saw Camilla on Demetrio's saddle, her face covered with blood.

Luis Cervantes hurried toward her with his medical supplies, but Camilla, choking down her sobs, wiped her eyes, and said hoarsely:

"You? Not even if I were dying!... Not even water!..."

In Cuquío, Demetrio received a message.

"Back to Tepatitlán, General," said Luis Cervantes, scanning the dispatch rapidly. "You've got to leave the men there while you go to Lagos and take the train over to Aguascalientes."

There was much heated protest. Some of the men from the sierra muttered and complained and swore that they wouldn't continue with the troop.

Camilla wept all night, and the next day, at dawn, she begged Demetrio to let her return home.

"If you don't like me ..." he answered sullenly.

"It's not that, Don Demetrio. I care for you a lot, really. But you've seen how it is.... That woman!..."

"Never mind about her. I'm going to send her the hell out of here today. I had already decided that."

Camilla dried her tears.

All the men were saddling up their horses. Demetrio went up to Pintada and said under his breath:

"You're not coming with us anymore."

"What!" she gasped.

"You can stay here or go wherever you damn well please, but not with us."

"What are you saying?" she exclaimed in astonishment. "You mean you're getting rid of me? Ha, ha, ha . . . Well, what the . . . What kind of a man are you if you believe that woman's gossip!"

And Pintada proceeded to insult Camilla, Demetrio, Luis Cervantes, and anyone else who came to mind, with such energy and originality that the soldiers heard insults and profanity they'd never even imagined.

Demetrio waited a long time patiently; she showed no sign of stopping, and he said to a soldier quite calmly:

"Throw this drunken woman out."

"Güero Margarito, love of my life! Come defend me from these . . . ! Come on, Güero dear. . . . Come show them you're a real man, and they're nothing but sons of a . . . !"

She gesticulated, kicked, and shouted.

Margarito appeared. He had just gotten up; his blue eyes were lost under his swollen eyelids; his voice was hoarse. He asked what was going on, and then he went up to Pintada, and with great seriousness, said:

"It's fine with me if you just get the hell out of here. We're all fed up with you!"

Pintada's face turned to granite. She tried to speak, but her muscles were rigid.

The soldiers laughed in great amusement. Camilla, terrified, held her breath.

Pintada stared at everyone about her. It all happened in the blink of an eye. She bent down, drew a sharp, gleaming blade from her stocking, and leapt at Camilla.

A shrill cry and a body falls, the blood gushing from it.

"Kill her," cried Demetrio, beside himself.

Two soldiers rushed at Pintada, but she brandished her dagger, defying them to touch her:

"Not you, you miserable . . . ! Kill me yourself, Demetrio!"

She stepped forward, handed over her dagger, thrust her breast forward, and let her arms fall to her side.

Demetrio picked up the dagger, red with blood, but his eyes clouded; he hesitated, took a step backward.

Then, with a low hoarse voice he growled:
"Get out of here! Now!"
No one dared stop her.
She moved off slowly, mute and somber.
Margarito's shrill, guttural voice broke the silent stupor:
"Thank God! . . . At last I'm rid of that louse!"

XIII

Someone plunged a knife
Deep in my side.
Did he know why?
I don't know why.
Surely he knew,
But not I . . .
The blood flowed out
Of that mortal wound.
Did he know why?
I don't know why.
Surely he knew,
But not I . . .

His head lowered, his hands crossed over the pommel of his saddle, Demetrio hummed the little tune over and over in a melancholy voice. Then he fell silent; long minutes passed, and he remained quiet and sorrowful.

"You'll see, as soon as we reach Lagos you'll come out of it, General. There's plenty of pretty girls to give us a good time," Güero Margarito said.

"Right now I just feel like getting drunk," Demetrio answered.

And he moved away from them, spurring his horse forward as if he wished to abandon himself entirely to his grief.

After many hours of riding, he called to Cervantes.

"Listen, Curro, why in the world am I going to Aguascalientes?"

"You have to vote for the Provisional President of the Republic, General!"[1]

"Provisional President? . . . What the devil, then, is Carranza? To tell the truth, I don't understand politics."

———

They arrived at Lagos. Güero bet that he would make Demetrio laugh that evening.

Trailing his spurs, his chaps sagging below his waist, Demetrio entered "El Cosmopolita" with Luis Cervantes, Güero Margarito, and his assistants.

"What are you running away from? . . . We won't eat you!" exclaimed Güero.

The townspeople, surprised in their attempt to escape, remained where they were. Some pretended they were returning to their tables to continue drinking and talking; others hesitantly stepped up to pay their respects to the commander.

"General, so pleased! . . . Major!"

"That's right! That's how I like my friends, refined and educated," Güero said. "Come on, boys," he added, jovially drawing his gun, "I'm going to play a tune that'll make you dance."

A bullet ricocheted on the cement floor, passing between the legs of the table and between the legs of the young gentlemen, who began to jump like a woman with a mouse caught in her skirts.

Pale as ghosts, they smile obsequiously at the major. Demetrio barely parts his lips, but his followers double over with laughter.

"Güero," Codorniz notices, "that man got stung. Look how he's limping."

Güero, without turning to look at the wounded man, announces with enthusiasm that he can shoot off the top of a tequila bottle at thirty paces without taking aim.

"Come on, friend, stand up," he says to the waiter. Then he drags him by the hand to the top of the hotel patio and sets a tequila bottle on his head.

The poor devil resists; frightened, he tries to escape, but Güero pulls his gun and takes aim.

"Get back in place ... stupid! Or I really will give you a hot one."

Güero goes to the opposite wall, raises his gun, and fires.

The bottle breaks into pieces, spilling tequila over the lad's deathly pale face.

"Now we're on a roll," he cries, running to the bar for another bottle to place on the lad's head.

He returns to the spot, whirls around, and shoots without aiming.

But he hits the waiter's ear instead of the bottle.

Holding his sides with laughter, he says to the young boy:

"Here, kid, take these bills. It's not so bad! You'll be all right with some brandy and a bit of arnica."

After drinking a great deal of alcohol and beer, Demetrio speaks up:

"Pay the bill, Güero. I'm leaving."

"I ain't got a penny, General, but don't worry about it.... How much do we owe you, friend?"

"One hundred and eighty pesos, chief," the bartender answers amiably.

Quickly, Güero jumps over the bar and, with a sweep of both arms, knocks down all the glasses and bottles.

"Send the bill to your papa Villa, understand?"

He heads out, laughing loudly at his prank.

"Say there, friend, where do the girls hang out?" he asks, reeling drunkenly toward a small well-dressed man who's closing the door of a tailor shop.

The man steps off the sidewalk politely to let him pass. Güero stops and looks at him curiously and impertinently.

"Listen, friend, you're very small and dainty, ain't you? ... No? ... Then I'm a liar? ... Fine with me. You know the dwarf dance? ... You don't? Sure you do! ... I met you in a circus! I swear you know how and real good too! ... You watch!"

Güero draws his gun and begins to shoot at the tailor's feet; the fat little man jumps at every pull of the trigger.

"See! You do know how to do the dwarf dance."

And throwing his arms over his friends' shoulders, he has them lead him to the red-light district, punctuating every step with shots at the corner streetlights, the doors, the houses. Demetrio leaves him and returns to the hotel, humming to himself:

> Someone plunged a knife
> Deep in my side.
> Did he know why?
> I don't know why.
> Surely he knew,
> But not I . . .

XIV

Cigar smoke, the acrid odor of sweaty clothing, the vapors of alcohol, the breathing of a crowd of people: worse by far than a trainful of pigs. Men in Texas hats, adorned with gold braid, and khaki suits predominate.

"Gentlemen, a well-dressed man stole my suitcase in the station at Silao. My life's savings! I haven't got enough to feed my little boy now!"

The voice was piercing, shrill and whining; but it was soon drowned out by the tumult within the train.

"What's the old woman talking about?" Güero asked, entering in search of a seat.

"Something about a suitcase ... and a well-dressed little boy ..." replied Pancracio, who had already found the laps of two civilians to sit on.

Demetrio and the others elbowed their way in. Since the ones who were supporting Pancracio preferred to leave their seats and stand, Demetrio and Luis Cervantes gladly took them.

A woman who had stood all the way from Irapuato, holding her child, fainted. A civilian took the child in his arms. The others pretended to have seen nothing. Some women, traveling with the soldiers, occupied two or three seats with baggage, dogs, cats, and parrots. Some of the men wearing Texas hats laughed at the heavy thighs and pendulous breasts of the woman who fainted.

"Gentlemen, a well-dressed man stole my suitcase in the station at Silao! All my life's savings . . . I haven't got enough to feed my little boy now! . . ."

The old woman speaks rapidly, parrotlike, sighing and sobbing. Her sharp eyes peer about on all sides. Here she gets a bill, and further on, another. They shower money upon her.

She finishes the collection, and goes a few seats ahead.

"Gentlemen, a well-dressed man stole my suitcase in the station at Silao!"

Her words produce an immediate and certain effect.

A well-dressed man! A well-dressed man, stealing a suitcase! Of all the low-down tricks! It awakens a feeling of universal indignation. What a pity that the well-dressed man isn't here right now so that every single one of the generals could shoot him!

"There's nothing as vile as a thieving city dude!" a man says, exploding with indignation.

"Robbing a poor old lady!"

"Stealing from a defenseless woman!"

They prove their compassion by word and deed: a harsh verdict against the culprit, a five-peso bill for the victim.

"To tell the truth," Güero Margarito declares, "I don't think it's wrong to kill, because when you kill, it's always out of anger. But stealing . . . Bah!"

This profound piece of reasoning meets with unanimous assent. But after a few moments of silence and thought, a colonel ventures his opinion:

"The truth is, everything has its whys and wherefores. Isn't that so? The honest truth is, I've stolen . . . and if I say that all of us here have done the same, I reckon I wouldn't be lying."

"Hell, I stole a lot of them sewing machines in Mexico," exclaimed a major. "I made more'n five hundred pesos even though I sold them at fifty cents apiece!"

A toothless, white-haired captain said:

"I stole some horses in Zacatecas, and such fine ones, that I said to myself, 'This is your own little lottery, Pascual Mata; you won't have a worry in all your life after this.' And the damned thing about it was that General Limón took a fancy to the horses, too, and he stole them from me!"

"Of course, there's no use denying it! I've stolen too," Güero Margarito agreed. "But ask any one of my partners how much profit I've got. I like to spend it on my friends. I have a better time drinking myself senseless than sending one red cent to the old women back home ..."

The subject of "I stole," though apparently inexhaustible, is running out of steam when decks of cards appear on the seats, drawing generals and officers as the light draws mosquitoes.

The excitement of gambling soon absorbs them all and heats up the atmosphere. They breathe in the barracks, the prison, the brothel, and even the pigsty.

And, rising above the babble, from the next car they hear the cry: "Gentlemen, a well-dressed man stole ..."

———

The streets in Aguascalientes had been turned into refuse piles. Men in khaki swarmed like bees around their hive, overrunning the restaurants, the cheap inns and eateries, the mess-hall tables, and the stands of the street vendors where rancid pork lay alongside a mountain of grimy cheese.

The smell of fried food whetted the appetites of Demetrio and his men. They forced their way into a small inn, where a disheveled, old hag served them, on earthenware plates, pork bones swimming in a clear chili broth and three tough, burnt tortillas. They paid two pesos apiece, and, as they left, Pancracio assured his comrades that he was hungrier than when he entered.

"Now," said Demetrio, "we'll go and consult General Natera!"

They made for the northern leader's billet.

A noisy, excited crowd stopped them at a street crossing. A man, buried in the multitude, was mouthing words in the monotonous, unctuous tones of a prayer. They came up close enough to see him distinctly. The man wore a shirt and trousers of coarse, white cloth, and he was repeating:

"All good Catholics who read this prayer to Christ Our Lord upon the Cross with due devotion will be immune from storms, pestilence, war, and famine."

"This man's no fool," said Demetrio, smiling.

The man waved a sheaf of printed handbills in his hand and cried:

"Fifty cents for this prayer to Christ Our Lord upon the Cross, just fifty cents ..."

Then he would disappear for a moment, to reappear with a snake's tooth, a sea star, or the skeleton of a fish. In the same singsong tone, he lauded the medicinal properties and the rare virtues of each article.

Codorniz, who had no faith in Venancio, asked the man to pull a tooth out; Güero purchased a black seed from a certain fruit that protected the possessor from lightning or any other catastrophe; and Anastasio Montañez purchased a prayer to Christ Our Lord upon the Cross, which he carefully folded up and proudly stuck into his shirt.

———

"As sure as there's a God in heaven, *compañero,*" Natera said, "the fighting hasn't blown over yet. Now it's Villa against Carranza."

Without answering him, his eyes wide open, Demetrio demanded a further explanation.

"It means," Natera insisted, "that the Convention won't recognize Carranza as First Chief of the Constitutionalist Army, and it's going to elect a Provisional President of the Republic. . . . Do you understand me, *compañero?*"

Demetrio nodded assent.

"What's your opinion, *compañero?*" asked Natera.

Demetrio shrugged his shoulders.

"It seems to me that the meat of the matter is that we've got to go on fighting. All right! Let's go to it! You know me, General, I'm game to the end."

"Good, but on what side?"

Demetrio, nonplussed, scratched his head:

"Look here, don't ask me any more questions. I never went to school, you know.... You gave me the eagle I wear on my hat, didn't you? ... All right then; you just tell me: 'Demetrio, do this or do that,' and that's all there is to it!"

PART THREE

"Villa? Oregón? Carranza? What do I care? ... I love the Revolution like I love the volcano that's erupting! The volcano because it's a volcano; the Revolution because it's the Revolution!"

I

EL PASO, TEXAS, MAY 16, 1915

MY DEAR VENANCIO,

Due to the pressure of professional duties, I have been unable to answer your letter of January 4 until now. As you already know, I gradu-
ated last December. I was sorry to hear of Pancracio's and Manteca's
fate, though I am not surprised that they stabbed each other over the
gambling table. It is a pity; they were both brave men. I am deeply
grieved not to be able to tell Güero Margarito how sincerely and
heartily I congratulate him for the only noble and beautiful thing he
ever did in his whole life: to have shot himself!

Dear Venancio, although you may have enough gold and silver to
purchase a degree, I am afraid you won't find it very easy to become a
doctor in the United States. You know I think highly of you, Venancio;
and I think you deserve a better fate. But I have an idea that may prove
favorable to our mutual interests and to your just ambition to improve
your social position. We could do a fine business here if we were to become partners. I have no reserve funds at the moment, since I've spent
all I had on my studies, but I have something much more valuable than
money: my perfect knowledge of this town and its needs and the kinds
of business that are sure to succeed. We could set up a typical Mexican
restaurant, with you as the owner, splitting the profits at the end of

each month. Furthermore, concerning a question that interests us both very much, namely, your social improvement, I remember that you play the guitar quite well; and, in view of the recommendations I could give you, and your training, as well, you might easily be admitted as a member of the Salvation Army, an extremely respectable group that would bring you no inconsiderable social prestige.

Don't hesitate, dear Venancio; come at once and bring your funds, and we'll get rich in no time. My best wishes to the General, to Anastasio, and the rest of the boys.

Your affectionate friend,
Luis Cervantes

Venancio finished reading the letter for the hundredth time and, sighing, repeated:

"That Curro certainly knows how to get things done!"

"What I can't get into my head," observed Anastasio Montañez, "is why we keep on fighting. Didn't we finish off this man Huerta and his Federation?"

Neither the General nor Venancio answered; but those words kept beating down on their dull brains like a hammer on an anvil.

They ascended the steep hill, their heads bowed, pensive, their horses walking at a slow gait. Restless and stubborn, Anastasio made the same observation to other groups of soldiers, who laughed at his candor. If a man has a rifle in his hands and a beltful of cartridges, it can be only for fighting. Against whom? For whom? That's never mattered to anyone!

The endless, wavering column of dust stretched out along the trail: a swirling anthill of broad, straw sombreros; dirty, old khaki; faded blankets; and the moving, black stain of the cavalry.

The men were dying of thirst. Not a pool or stream or well anywhere along the road. A wave of heat rose from the white, wild sides of a small canyon, throbbed above the hoary crest of huisache trees and the greenish stumps of cactus. Like a jest, the cactus flowers opened, some fresh, fleshy, bright red; others pointed and transparent.

At noon they stumbled upon a hut clinging to the precipitous sierra, then three more huts strewn along the banks of a river of burnt sand; but everything was silent, desolate. As soon as they saw the troops, the people scurried into the hills to hide.

Demetrio grew indignant.

"Bring me anyone you find hiding or running away," he commanded in a loud voice.

"What? What did you say?" Valderrama cried in surprise. "The men of the sierra? These brave men who haven't acted like those chickens down in Zacatecas and Aguascalientes? Our own brothers, who weather storms, clinging to the rocks like moss itself? I protest, señor; I protest!"

He spurred his miserable horse forward and caught up with the General.

"The men of the sierra," he said solemnly and emphatically, "are flesh of our flesh, bone of our bone. *Os ex osibus meis et caro de carne mea.* Mountaineers are made from the same timber we're made of! Of the same sound timber from which heroes are carved...."

With a confidence as sudden as it was courageous, he hit the General across the chest. The General smiled benevolently.

Valderrama, the tramp, the crazy poet, did he know what he was saying?

When the soldiers reached a small ranch and milled desperately around the empty huts and small houses, without finding a single stale tortilla, a solitary rotten pepper, or one pinch of salt to flavor the horrible taste of dry meat, the owners of the huts, their peaceful brethren, watched from their hideouts—some with the stone-like impassivity of Aztec idols; others, more human, with a slow smile on their colorless lips and beardless faces—how those fierce men, who less than a month ago had made the miserable huts of others tremble with fear, now were leaving their huts where ovens were cold and water tanks dry, fleeing with their tails between their legs, cringing, like curs kicked out of their own houses.

But the General did not countermand his order, and a few soldiers brought back four fugitives, captive and bound.

II

"Why are you hiding?" Demetrio asked the prisoners.

"We're not hiding, chief, we're just following the trail."

"Where to?"

"To our own homes, in God's name, to Durango."

"Is this the road to Durango?"

"Peaceful folk can't travel over the main road, nowadays, you know that, chief."

"You're not peaceful folk, you're deserters. Where do you come from?" Demetrio insisted, eyeing them with keen scrutiny.

The prisoners grew confused; they looked at one another bewildered, unable to give a prompt answer.

"They're Carranzistas," one of the soldiers observed.

That brought the prisoners back to their senses. It cleared up the mystery of who the unknown troops could be.

"Carranzistas, us?" one of them answered proudly. "I'd rather be a pig."

"The truth is we're deserters," another said. "After the defeat, we deserted from General Villa's troops this side of Celaya."[1]

"General Villa defeated? Ha! Ha!"

The soldiers laughed.

But Demetrio's brow was wrinkled as though a black shadow had passed before his eyes.

"The son of a . . . hasn't been born who can beat General Villa!" a bronzed veteran with a scar clear across his face claimed insolently.

Without changing expression, one of the deserters stared persistently at him and said:

"I know who you are. When we took Torreón, you were with General Urbina. In Zacatecas you were with General Natera and then you shifted to the Jalisco troops. Am I lying?"

These words met with a sudden and definite effect. The prisoners gave a detailed account of the tremendous defeat of Villa at Celaya.

Demetrio's men listened in a stupefied silence.

Before resuming their march, they built a fire to roast some bull meat. Anastasio Montañez, searching for firewood among the huisache trees, glimpsed the close-cropped neck of Valderrama's horse in the distance, among the rocks.

"Hey! Come on out, you fool, there wasn't any bloodshed after all!" he shouted.

Because Valderrama, the romantic poet, could disappear for a whole day whenever there was talk of shooting someone.

Valderrama heard Anastasio's voice, and he must have been convinced that the prisoners had been set at liberty, because moments later he joined Venancio and Demetrio.

"Heard the news?" Venancio asked gravely.

"No."

"It's very serious. A disaster! Villa was beaten at Celaya by Obregón. Carranza is winning all along the line! We're done for!"

Valderrama's gesture was as disdainful and solemn as an emperor's.

"Villa? Obregón? Carranza? What do I care? . . . I love the Revolution like I love the volcano that's erupting! The volcano because it's a volcano; the Revolution because it's the Revolution! . . . But the stones left above or below after the cataclysm? What are they to me?"

And because, in the glare of the midday sun, the reflection of a white tequila bottle glittered, he turned tail and ran jubilantly toward the bearer of such a marvelous gift.

"I like this crazy fool," Demetrio said with a smile. "He says things sometimes that make you think."

They resumed their march; their uneasiness translated into a lugubrious silence. Slowly, inevitably, the other catastrophe was unfolding. Villa defeated was a fallen god. And fallen gods are not gods at all, they are nothing.

When Codorniz spoke, his words faithfully captured the general opinion:

"What the hell, boys! . . . Every spider's got to spin his own web now!"

III

In Zacatecas and Aguascalientes, the little country towns and the neighboring communities, haciendas, and ranches were deserted.

When one of the officers found a barrel of tequila, the event assumed miraculous proportions. Everything was conducted with secrecy and care; deep mystery was preserved and the soldiers were obliged to leave the next day, before sunrise, under the charge of Anastasio and Venancio. When Demetrio awoke to the strains of music, his general staff, now composed chiefly of young ex-government officers, told him of the discovery, and Codorniz, interpreting the thoughts of his colleagues, said sententiously:

"These are bad times and you've got to take advantage of everything. If there are some days when a duck can swim, there are others when he can't even take a drink."

The string musicians played all day; the most solemn honors were paid to the barrel; but Demetrio was very sad, and he kept repeating his refrain.

"Did he know why?
I don't know why."

In the afternoon there were cockfights. Demetrio sat down with the chief officers under the roof of the municipal portals, in front of a city square covered with weeds, a tumbled kiosk, and some abandoned adobe houses.

"Valderrama," Demetrio called, looking away from the ring in boredom, "come and sing me a song ... sing 'The Gravedigger.'"

But Valderrama did not hear him, because, instead of watching the fight, he was reciting an impassioned soliloquy as he watched the sunset over the hills. With solemn gestures and emphatic tones, he said:

"O Lord, Lord, pleasurable is this Thy land! I shall build me three tents: one for Thee, one for Moses, one for Elijah!"

"Valderrama," Demetrio shouted again. "Come and sing 'The Gravedigger' for me."

"Hey, crazy, the General is calling you," an officer called him over.

And Valderrama, with his eternally complacent smile, went over and asked the musicians for a guitar.

"Silence," the gamesters cried.

Valderrama finished tuning his instrument. Codorniz and Meco let loose on the sand a pair of cocks armed with long sharp blades attached to their legs. One was light red; his feathers shone with beautiful obsidian glints. The other was sand-colored, with feathers like scales burnt to a fiery copper color.

The fight was swift, and as fierce as a duel between men. As though moved by springs, the roosters flew at each other. Their necks arched and tense, their coral-colored eyes, their combs erect, their legs taut; for an instant they hung in the air without even touching the ground, their feathers, beaks, and claws lost in a dizzy whirlwind. The red rooster suddenly broke loose, tossed outside the chalk lines with his legs to heaven. His vermilion eyes flickered out, his leathery eyelids closed slowly, his puffed-up feathers shuddered convulsively in a pool of blood.

Valderrama, who could not repress a gesture of violent indignation, began to play. With the first melancholy strains of the tune, his anger disappeared. His eyes gleamed with the light of madness. His glance strayed over the square, the tumbled kiosk, the old adobe houses, with the mountains in the background, and the sky, burning like a roof afire. He began to sing.

He put such feeling into his voice and such expression into the strings that, as he finished, Demetrio turned his head aside so they couldn't see his eyes.

But Valderrama fell upon him, embraced him warmly, and with the same familiarity he showed everyone at the appropriate moment, he whispered:

"Drink them! . . . Those are beautiful tears."

Demetrio asked for the bottle, passed it to Valderrama.

Greedily the poet drank half its contents in one gulp; then, showing only the whites of his eyes, he faced the spectators dramatically and, in a highly theatrical voice, cried:

"Here you may witness the pleasures of the Revolution caught in a single tear."

Then he continued talking like a madman, completely mad, with the dusty weeds, the tumbled kiosk, the gray houses, the proud hill, and the immeasurable sky.

IV

Juchipila appeared in the distance, white and bathed in sunlight, in the midst of a thick forest at the foot of a proud, lofty mountain, pleated like a turban.

Some of the soldiers, gazing at the church spires, sighed sadly. Now their march through the canyons was the march of a blind man without his guide; they tasted the bitterness of exodus.

"Is that town Juchipila?" Valderrama asked.

Valderrama, just getting started on the day's first binge, had been counting the crosses scattered along the road, along the trails, in the hollows near the rocks, in the rugged streambeds, and along the riverbanks. Crosses of black timber newly varnished, makeshift crosses built out of two logs, crosses of piled up stones, crosses whitewashed on crumbling walls, humble crosses drawn with charcoal on the surface of whitish rocks. The trace of the blood shed by the first revolutionaries of 1910, murdered by the Government.

With Juchipila in full view, Valderrama gets off his horse, bends down, kneels, and gravely kisses the ground.

The soldiers pass by without stopping. Some laugh at the crazy man, others crack a joke. Valderrama, deaf to all about him, solemnly recites his prayer:

"O Juchipila, cradle of the Revolution of 1910, O blessed land, land steeped in the blood of martyrs, blood of dreamers, the only truly good men ..."

"Because they had no time to be bad!" an ex–Federal officer brutally finishes the thought as he rides by.

Valderrama interrupts his prayer, thinks, frowns, knits his brow, breaks into a loud laugh that echoes off the rocks, and saddles up and chases after the officer, asking him for a swallow of tequila.

Soldiers missing an arm or leg, cripples, rheumatics, and consumptives speak bitterly of Demetrio. Young upstarts, armchair warriors, wear their officers' stripes on their hats, even before they know how to handle a rifle; while the veteran, exhausted in a hundred battles, now incapacitated for work, the veteran who had set out as a simple private, is still a private.

The few remaining officers among Demetrio's friends also grumble, because his staff is now made up of young gentlemen from the capital, perfumed and neatly dressed.

"The worst part of it," Venancio says, "is that we're getting overcrowded with Federals!"

Anastasio himself, who invariably has only praise for Demetrio's conduct, now seems to share the general discontent.

"See here, *compañeros*," he exclaims, "I'm plainspoken ... and always tell the boss that if these people stick to us very long we'll be in a hell of a fix. Certainly! How can anyone think otherwise? I don't mince words; and by the mother that bore me, I'm going to tell Demetrio so myself."

And he told him. Demetrio listened benevolently, and, when Anastasio had finished, he replied:

"Compadre, you're absolutely right. We're in a bad way: the privates complain about the corporals, the corporals complain about the officers, and the officers complain about us.... And we're all about ready to send both Villa and Carranza to hell to have a good time all by themselves. ... I guess we're in the same fix as that peon from Tepatitlán who complained about his boss all day long, but he never stopped working for him. That's us. We kick and kick, but we keep on killing and killing. But it's best not to say anything, compadre."

"Why, Demetrio?"

"Hm, I don't know.... Because it is ... do you see? ... What we've got to do is to raise the men's spirits. I've got orders to stop a band of men coming through Cuquío, see? In a few days we'll have to fight the Carranzistas; and this time we better give them a beating."

Valderrama, the highway tramp, who had enlisted in Demetrio's army one day, without anyone remembering exactly when or where, overheard some of Demetrio's words, and because not even a fool eats fire, that very day Valderrama disappeared just as he had arrived.

V

They entered the streets of Juchipila as the church bells rang, loud and joyfully, with that peculiar tone that thrills all the people of that region.

"It makes me think we are back in the days when the revolution was just beginning, when the bells rang like mad in every town we entered and everybody came out with music, flags, cheers, and fireworks to welcome us," said Anastasio Montañez.

"They don't like us anymore," Demetrio returned.

"Of course, because we're crawling back like a dog with its tail between its legs," Codorniz remarked.

"It ain't that, I guess. They don't give a damn for the other side either."

"But why should they like us, compadre?"

They spoke no more.

They poured into the city square in front of a rough, massive, octagonal church, reminiscent of colonial times.

At one time the square must have been a garden, judging from the bare, stunted orange trees planted between iron and wooden benches.

The sonorous, joyful bells rang again. From within the church, the honeyed voices of a female chorus rose, melancholy and grave. To the strains of a guitar, the young girls of the town sang the "Mysteries."

"What's the fiesta, lady?" Venancio asked of an old woman who was running toward the church.

"The Sacred Heart of Jesus!" answered the pious woman, panting.

They remembered that one year ago they had captured Zacatecas. They all grew sadder still. Juchipila, like the other towns they had passed through on their way from Tepic, by way of Jalisco, Aguascalientes, and Zacatecas, was in ruins. The black trail of the fires showed in the roofless houses, in the charred railings.

Shuttered houses; and here and there an open store offered a sarcastic sneer, showing its empty shelves like the white skeletons of horses strewn along the roads. The grimace of hunger was on every dusty face, in the smoldering eyes that blazed with hatred when they met a soldier's glance.

In vain the soldiers scour the streets in search of food, biting their lips in anger. A single lunchroom is open; at once they fill it. No beans, no tortillas, only chili and salt. In vain, the officers show their pocketbooks stuffed with bills, or try to use threats.

"Yeah, you've got papers, all right! That's all you've brought! Try and eat them, will you?" says the owner, an insolent old shrew with an enormous scar on her cheek, who tells them she had "already slept with a dead man" to cure her from ever feeling frightened again.

And in the melancholy and desolation of the town, while the women sing in the church, birds chirp in the grove and the thrushes pipe their lyrical strain on the withered branches of the orange trees.

VI

Demetrio Macías's wife, mad with joy, rushed along the trail to meet him, leading a child by the hand.

An absence of almost two years!

They embraced each other and stood speechless; she overcome with sobs and tears.

Demetrio stared in astonishment at his wife, who seemed to have aged ten or twenty years. Then he looked at the child, who fixed his eyes on him in terror. His heart leapt to his mouth, as he saw in the child his own steely features and fiery eyes, exactly reproduced. He wanted to hold him in his arms, but the frightened little boy took refuge in his mother's skirts.

"It's your own father, baby! . . . It's your daddy!"

The child hid his face within the folds of his mother's skirts, still too shy.

Demetrio handed the reins of his horse to his orderly and walked slowly along the steep trail with his wife and son.

"Thank God you've come back! . . . Now you'll never leave us anymore, will you? . . . You'll stay with us always?"

Demetrio's face clouded over.

Both remained silent, lost in anguish.

A black cloud rose behind the sierra, and a deafening roar of thunder was heard. Demetrio suppressed a sigh. Memories swarmed into his mind like bees around a hive.

The rain began to fall in heavy drops; they took shelter in a rocky little cave.

The rain came pelting down, shaking the white St. John's roses like handfuls of stars caught on the trees, the rocks, the bushes, and the pitahayas all over the mountainside.

Below, in the depths of the canyon, through the gauze of the rain, they could see the tall, swaying palms; slowly their crowns were swinging in the wind and opening out like fans.

Everywhere, mountains, heaving hills, more hills, and beyond, locked amid mountains, more mountains encircled by the wall of the sierra, with peaks so high that their blue summits vanished in the sapphire of the sky.

"Demetrio, for God's sake! . . . Don't go away! . . . My heart is warning me something will happen to you this time."

Again she is wracked with sobs.

The child, frightened, cries and screams, and she has to control her own great grief to calm him.

Gradually the rain stops; a swallow, with silver breast and angled wings, cuts across the silver threads of the rain, gleaming suddenly in the afternoon sunshine.

"Why do you keep on fighting, Demetrio?"

Demetrio, frowning deeply, absentmindedly picks up a small stone and throws it to the bottom of the canyon. He stares pensively over the precipice and says:

"Look at that stone; how it keeps on going. . . ."

VII

It was a heavenly morning. It had rained all night, and the sky dawned covered with a canopy of white clouds. Young, wild colts trotted on the summit of the sierra, with streaming manes and out-stretched tails, graceful as the elegant peaks that lift their heads to kiss the clouds.

The soldiers step along the steep crags, buoyed up by the happiness of the morning. No one thinks of the treacherous bullet that might be awaiting him up ahead; the unforeseen provides man with his greatest joy. The soldiers sing, laugh, and chatter away. The spirit of ancient nomadic tribes stirs their souls. No one cares to know where they are going, or where they are coming from. All that matters is to walk, to walk endlessly, without ever stopping; to possess the valley, the mountain plains, far as the eye can reach.

Trees, brush, and cactus shine, freshly washed. Heavy drops of limpid water spill from rocks as ocher in hue as rusty armor.

Demetrio Macías's men grow silent for a moment. They think they've heard a familiar sound, the distant firing of a rocket; but a few minutes elapse, and nothing more is heard.

"In this same sierra," Demetrio says, "with just twenty men I killed five hundred Federals."

As Demetrio begins to tell that famous exploit, the men realize the danger they are facing. What if the enemy, instead of being two days away, is hiding somewhere among the underbrush in the terrible ravine, along whose floor they now advanced? But which one would show his fear? When did Demetrio Macías's men ever say "we won't go there"?

So, when firing begins in the distance, where the guard is marching, no one feels surprised. The recruits turn tail in a reckless flight, searching for a way out of the canyon.

A curse breaks from Demetrio's parched throat.

"Fire at 'em. Shoot any man who runs away!

"Storm the hill!" he roars like a wild beast.

But the enemy, lying in ambush by the thousand, open up their machine-gun fire and Demetrio's men fall like wheat under the sickle.

Demetrio sheds tears of rage and pain when Anastasio slowly slides from his horse without a sound and lies outstretched, motionless. Venancio falls close beside him, his chest horribly riddled with bullets, and Meco hurtles over the precipice and rolls to the bottom of the abyss.

Suddenly, Demetrio finds himself alone. Bullets whiz past his ears like hail. He dismounts, drags himself over the rocks until he finds a parapet, positions a stone to protect his head, and, lying flat on the ground, begins to shoot.

The enemy scatter in all directions, pursuing the few fugitives hiding in the brush.

Demetrio aims; he does not miss with a single shot. Bang! . . . Bang! . . . Bang!

His famous marksmanship fills him with joy. Wherever he settles his glance, he settles a bullet. He loads his gun once more . . . takes aim. . . .

The smoke of the guns hangs thick in the air. Locusts chant their mysterious, imperturbable song; doves coo lyrically in the crannies of the rocks; the cows graze placidly.

The sierra is clad in gala colors. Over its inaccessible peaks, the opalescent fog settles like a snowy veil on the forehead of a bride.

At the foot of a crevice, as huge and magnificent as the portico of an old cathedral, Demetrio Macías, his eyes fixed in an eternal stare, continues to point the barrel of his gun. . . .

NOTES

PART ONE

CHAPTER I

1. *Federals:* The Federals in the time frame of the novel are the government soldiers under the control of the newly installed dictator, Victoriano Huerta. See note for Chapter VIII for additional information on Huerta.
2. *Virgin of Jalpa:* The Virgin of Jalpa is venerated in the state of Jalisco, where the action of the novel takes place.

CHAPTER II

1. cacique: This Spanish word of indigenous etymology means "chief," and in Mexico it refers to the powerful landowners who were the "bosses," or the "chief authorities," in their town or region in the nineteenth and early twentieth centuries. They exercised great control over the economy and the lives of the local people. The term almost invariably connotes an abusive wielding of power.
2. *pitahayas:* The pitahaya is a climbing cactus with red or white flowers and an edible fruit. It is also spelled "pitaya."
3. *Julián Medina:* Medina was the governor of Jalisco, and an important ally of Francisco Villa. One of his famous deeds in the struggle against Huerta was his defeat of Federal soldiers in the town of Hostotipaquillo in May 1913. Azuela patterned Demetrio Macías in large part on Medina.

4. *Codorniz:* A number of the main characters in the novel have nicknames that characterize them in some significant or humorous way. I have left these names in Spanish in the translation. *Codorniz* is the Spanish word for "quail"; *manteca* means "lard" or "fat." Both nouns are feminine in Spanish, a fact that is emphasized in the original text by the inclusion of the definite article as part of their names when the narrator refers to them: *la Codorniz* and *la Manteca.*

CHAPTER IV

1. The Wandering Jew ... The May Sun: *The Wandering Jew* was a popular nineteenth-century novel, written by Eugène Sue (1804–57); *The May Sun* is a historical novel about the French intervention in Mexico, written by the popular Mexican novelist Juan Antonio Mateos (1831–1913).

CHAPTER V

1. curro: *Curro* is a derogatory term meaning "tenderfoot" or "dandy." It refers to someone who is from the city, refined and elegant, and not experienced in country life. A *curro* is not one of *los de abajo.* The nickname "Curro" is given to Luis Cervantes, and used by all of Demetrio Macías's men.
2. mochos: A derogatory term used for the Federal soldiers and connoting cowardice. The literal meanings of *mocho* include a person who is missing a limb, and a bull with its horns clipped off.

CHAPTER VI

1. *Virgin of Guadalupe:* The most important apparition of the Virgin Mary in Mexico, and perhaps in all of the Americas, was reported during colonial times and involved the Virgin's miraculous appearance before an indigenous man, Juan Diego. The Virgin of Guadalupe is the patron saint of Mexico, and she is venerated throughout the country.

CHAPTER VIII

1. *Huerta's protestations:* The Mexican Revolution of 1910 started as a movement against the more than thirty-year dictatorship of Porfirio Díaz. Francisco I. Madero, the son of wealthy landowners, ran as an opposition candidate to Díaz in the 1910 elections, with the political program of effective suffrage and no reelection of the president ("Sufragio efectivo, no reelección"). The results of the election were widely understood to be fraudulent, and Díaz was rather quickly overthrown by a loose coalition of revolutionary leaders temporarily united behind

Madero. Madero became president in 1911. Mariano Azuela was himself a supporter of the new regime.

Victoriano Huerta, an army general since the times of Díaz and opposed to the new government, led a revolt and had Madero arrested on February 13, 1913, and assassinated on February 21. He assumed power as a military dictator. The other revolutionary leaders immediately opposed Huerta as a traitor to the elected president and an illegitimate head of state.

The time frame of the novel is roughly 1913–15, a period of armed combat throughout Mexico as the various factions involved in the Revolution fought against Huerta's army. The novel focuses on troops allied with Francisco Villa and narrates several of their important victories. Huerta resigned in July 1914 and was assassinated soon after. The novel covers the period immediately after this turning point as well.

CHAPTER IX
1. *Cofradía:* This is a Catholic religious organization of lay membership.

CHAPTER XI
1. *'La Adelita':* One of the most famous of the *corridos* (ballads) of the Mexican Revolution, "La Adelita" was a favorite among Villa's soldiers.

CHAPTER XII
1. *Pánfilo Natera:* Natera was a revolutionary general and another of Villa's allies. The fall of Zacatecas, a Huerta stronghold, was a significant defeat for the government.

CHAPTER XIII
1. *Félix or Felipe Díaz:* The confusion over the first name of Félix Díaz is another indication, like the mispronunciation of Carranza as "Carranzo" earlier in the novel (see p. 17), of the revolutionary soldiers' ignorance of their country's politics. Félix Díaz, nephew of Porfirio Díaz, and an aspiring politician throughout his life, opposed Madero and later opposed Carranza. He was linked in the popular imagination with the assassination of Madero.
2. *Villa . . . Carranza:* Francisco Villa and Venustiano Carranza were among the most powerful of the revolutionary generals fighting against Huerta. Carranza named himself *Primer Jefe* (First Chief) of Mexico after the defeat of Huerta. He ruled as president of Mexico from 1917 to 1920. His initial assumption of power in 1914 led to further violent opposition on the part of leaders, including Villa, who did not support

him for the presidency. In the novel, Demetrio's men go from fighting against the Federals to fighting against the Carranzistas, the troops controlled by Carranza.

CHAPTER XV

1. atole: *Atole* is a hot beverage made of corn.
2. *Obregón . . . Carrera Torres:* Alvaro Obregón, an ally of Villa in the fight against Huerta, later broke with Villa and supported Carranza in his bid for power. Guadalajara was an important stronghold for the Carranzistas, and a key target in Villa's military strategy. Francisco S. Carrera Torres was a general in the anti-Huerta fight.
3. *Tecolote:* This is another nickname, meaning "owl." *Tecolote* is also a slang term for "policeman."

CHAPTER XVI

1. *Ciudadela:* Military cadets were among the troops that rebelled against the Madero government in February 1913. (See note for Chapter VIII.) On the first day of the ten-day rebellion, called the *"decena trágica,"* the rebellious troops were forced to retreat to the Ciudadela, an old citadel on the south side of central Mexico City. General Aureliano Blanquet, to whom the young captain in the novel imagines writing a boastful letter, was in charge of the arrest of Madero on February 13.

PART TWO

CHAPTER I

1. charro: The *charro* suit is the traditional dress of Mexican horsemen (cowboys), consisting of elaborately decorated close-fitting pants and cropped jacket, a serape, and a broad-brimmed hat.
2. *Pintada . . . Güero Margarito:* Two of the main characters of the central section of the novel are introduced here. The name Güero Margarito means "blond" or "fair-haired Margarito." *Pintada* refers to a woman who is heavily rouged or "painted," and is a term connoting coarseness and sexual boldness.

CHAPTER V

1. *Antonio Plaza:* Plaza was a very popular Mexican poet in the late nineteenth and early twentieth centuries.

CHAPTER VIII

1. *Orozco:* Pascual Orozco was a revolutionary leader who supported Madero initially, but turned against him in 1912, in part over the issue of land reform. He later led counterrevolutionary forces against Villa.

CHAPTER IX
1. *Church's Rights:* The *fueros,* or Church rights and privileges in Mexico, inherited from colonial times, were abolished under the Reform governments of the nineteenth century, but tolerated by Porfirio Díaz, who did not enforce the Reform legislation. The clergy was strongly opposed to the Revolution, as a threat to their privilege and their power over education, land, banking, politics, and social norms.

CHAPTER XI
1. *Aguascalientes:* Carranza, having named himself *Primer Jefe* of Mexico, called a convention to be held in the city of Aguascalientes in November 1914. He expected his leadership to be legitimized at the convention, but Villa played a critical role in defeating Carranza's bid for the presidency.

CHAPTER XIII
1. *Provisional President of the Republic:* At the Aguascalientes Convention, Eulalio Gutiérrez, with the support of Villa, was elected Provisional President of Mexico, in opposition to Carranza's ambitions.

PART THREE
CHAPTER II
1. *Celaya:* The April 15, 1915, defeat of Villa at Celaya, in the state of Guanajuato, represented a crushing blow to the revolutionary general, the "Mexican Napoleon," at the hands of Alvaro Obregón.

FURTHER READING

MEXICAN REVOLUTION OF 1910

Aguilar Camín, Héctor, and Lorenzo Meyer. *In the Shadow of the Mexican Revolution: Contemporary Mexican History, 1910–1989.* Austin: University of Texas Press, 1993.

Benjamin, Thomas. *La Revolución: Mexico's Great Revolution as Memory, Myth and History.* Austin: University of Texas Press, 2000.

Brenner, Anita. *The Wind That Swept Mexico.* 1943. Reprint, Austin: University of Texas Press, 1985.

Hart, John Mason. *Revolutionary Mexico: The Coming and Process of the Mexican Revolution.* University of California Press, 1987.

Katz, Friedrich. *The Life and Times of Pancho Villa.* Stanford: Stanford University Press, 1998.

Knight, Alan. *The Mexican Revolution.* 2 vols. Cambridge: Cambridge University Press, 1986.

Krauze, Enrique. *Mexico: Biography of Power: A History of Modern Mexico, 1810–1996.* New York: HarperCollins, 1997.

Reed, John. *Insurgent Mexico.* 1914. Reprint, New York: Penguin Books, 1983.

MARIANO AZUELA AND *LOS DE ABAJO*

Bradley, D. "Patterns of Myth in *Los de abajo.*" *Modern Language Review* 75 (1980): 94-1–4.

Duffey, J. Patrick. "A War of Words: Orality and Literacy in Mariano Azuela's *Los de abajo.*" *Romance Notes* 38.2 (Winter 1998): 173–78.

Griffin, Clive. "The Structure of *Los de abajo.*" *Revista Canadiense de Estudios Hispánicos* 6.1 (Autumn 1981): 25–41.

Robe, Stanley L. *Azuela and the Mexican Underdogs.* Berkeley: University of California Press, 1979.

Rutherford, John. "The Novel of the Mexican Revolution." *The Cambridge History of Latin American Literature.* Vol. 2. Edited by Roberto González Echevarría and Enrique Pupo-Walker. Cambridge: Cambridge University Press, 1996.

A NOTE ON THE TYPE

The principal text of this Modern Library edition
was set in a digitized version of Janson,
a typeface that dates from about 1690 and was cut by Nicholas Kis,
a Hungarian working in Amsterdam. The original matrices have
survived and are held by the Stempel foundry in Germany.
Hermann Zapf redesigned some of the weights and sizes for Stempel,
basing his revisions on the original design.

MODERN LIBRARY IS ONLINE AT
WWW.MODERNLIBRARY.COM

MODERN LIBRARY ONLINE IS YOUR GUIDE
TO CLASSIC LITERATURE ON THE WEB

THE MODERN LIBRARY E-NEWSLETTER

Our free e-mail newsletter is sent to subscribers, and features sample chapters, interviews with and essays by our authors, upcoming books, special promotions, announcements, and news.

To subscribe to the Modern Library e-newsletter, send a blank e-mail to: sub_modernlibrary@info.randomhouse.com or visit www.modernlibrary.com

THE MODERN LIBRARY WEBSITE

Check out the Modern Library website at
www.modernlibrary.com for:

- The Modern Library e-newsletter
- A list of our current and upcoming titles and series
- Reading Group Guides and exclusive author spotlights
- Special features with information on the classics and other paperback series
- Excerpts from new releases and other titles
- A list of our e-books and information on where to buy them
- The Modern Library Editorial Board's 100 Best Novels and 100 Best Nonfiction Books of the Twentieth Century written in the English language
- News and announcements

Questions? E-mail us at modernlibrary@randomhouse.com
For questions about examination or desk copies, please visit
the Random House Academic Resources site at
www.randomhouse.com/academic

Fyodor Dostoevsky
THE BEST SHORT STORIES
Translated, and with an Introduction, by David Magarshack
Trade Paperback; $10.95 / C$16.95
0-375-75688-4

Alexandre Dumas
THE THREE MUSKETEERS
Translated by Jacques Le Clercq
Introduction by Alan Furst
Trade Paperback; $9.95 / C$14.95
0-375-75674-4

Gustave Flaubert
THE TEMPTATION OF SAINT ANTHONY
Translated by Lafcadio Hearn
Introduction by Michel Foucault
Trade Paperback; $13.95 / C$21.00
0-375-75912-3

Victor Hugo
THE HUNCHBACK OF NOTRE-DAME
Revised translation and Notes by Catherine Liu
Introduction by Elizabeth McCracken
Trade Paperback; $11.95 / C$17.95
0-679-64257-9

Victor Hugo
THE TOILERS OF THE SEA
Translated, and with Notes, by James Hogarth
Introduction by Graham Robb
Trade Paperback; $12.95 / C$14.95
0-375-76132-2

Martial
EPIGRAMS
Selected and translated by James Michie
Introduction by Shadi Bartsch
Trade Paperback; $13.95 / NCR
0-375-76042-3

Friedrich Nietzsche
BASIC WRITINGS
Translated, and with
Notes and edited by Walter Kaufmann
Introduction by Peter Gay
Commentary by major writers
Trade Paperback; $14.95 / C$22.95
0-679-78339-3

Ovid
THE ART OF LOVE
Translated by James Michie
Introduction by David Malouf
Trade Paperback; $11.95 / C$17.95
0-375-76117-9

THE TRAVELS OF MARCO POLO
Edited, and revised from William Marsden's translation, by Manuel Komroff
Introduction by Jason Goodwin
Trade Paperback; $13.95 / C$21.00
0-375-75818-6

THE SONG OF ROLAND
Translated and with an Introduction by W. S. Merwin
Trade Paperback; $8.95 / NCR
0-375-75711-2

Stendhal
THE CHARTERHOUSE OF PARMA
Translated by Richard Howard
Trade Paperback; $11.95 / C$17.95
0-679-78318-0

Leo Tolstoy
ANNA KARENINA
The Constance Garnett translation revised by
Leonard J. Kent and Nina Berberova
Introduction by Mona Simpson
Commentary by major writers
Trade Paperback; $9.95 / C$14.95
0-679-78330-X

Leo Tolstoy
CHILDHOOD, BOYHOOD, AND YOUTH
Translated and with an Introduction by Michael Scammell
Trade Paperback; $13.95 / C$21.00
0-375-75944-1

Leo Tolstoy
THE DEATH OF IVAN ILYITCH AND MASTER AND MAN
Translated by Constance Garnett
Introduction and Notes by Ann Pasternak Slater
Trade Paperback; $9.95 / C$14.95
0-375-76099-7

Leo Tolstoy
WAR AND PEACE
Translated by Constance Garnett
Introduction by A. N. Wilson
Trade Paperback; $13.95 / C$21.00
0-375-76064-4

Ivan Turgenev
FATHERS AND SONS
The Constance Garnett translation revised by Elizabeth Cheresh Allen
Introduction and Notes by Ann Pasternak Slater
Trade Paperback; $10.95 / C$16.95
0-375-75839-9

Jules Verne
THE MYSTERIOUS ISLAND
Translated by Jordan Stump
Introduction by Caleb Carr
Trade Paperback; $12.95 / C$19.95
0-8129-6642-2

Available at your bookstore or call toll-free to order: 1-800-733-3000.
Credit cards only. Prices subject to change.
www.modernlibrary.com